The Baumgartners Plus One
By Selena Kitt

eXcessica publishing

The Baumgartners Plus One © 2011 by Selena Kitt

Excessica LLC
486 S. Ripley #164
Alpena MI 49707

To order additional copies of this book, contact:
books@excessicapublishing.com
www.excessica.com

Cover art © 2015 Taria Reed
First Edition January 2011

Prologue

I met the Baumgartners because, as my mother was too fond of saying, "Danielle is nosier than a cat in a tuna fish factory." Maybe that was true and maybe it wasn't. But what was I supposed to do when someone started sunbathing nude right outside my back door—just close the blinds?

Besides, a fully-clothed Carrie Baumgartner would have been pretty hard to ignore, let alone a topless, unbelievably bronze one, completely covered in coconut-scented oil. The stuff was so strong I could smell it from the window.

I'd seen her around before—we waved to each other on the way to the mailbox, had even said, "Hi," and had brief conversations about having to lug laundry across the street and guests parking in our reserved spots—the usual neighbor stuff.

Maybe if I'd been a prude, or if I'd had kids like everyone else in University of Michigan married housing, or if Carrie had been just a little less attractive in her black bikini bottoms, I might have called campus security or just turned a blind eye like a good girl. But I didn't.

Instead, I was a very bad girl.

It had been a long time since I'd even thought about anyone sexually, but I had to admit, she perked my formerly dormant libido. She was so sexy, even fully clothed just passing me on the way to the mailbox, that her presence alone bordered on pornography. She probably would have made a ninety-year-old man remember what other function his cock was made to perform, aside from peeing the bed. She certainly made me wish for a moment that I had one myself, just so I could imagine it inside of her.

I knelt up on my bed—*our* bed still, not that Mason came home to it much anymore—and peeked around the white sheet I'd tacked to the wall as a curtain when we moved in. According to our lease, we were supposed to cover our windows and I'd just never gotten around to putting up the blinds. Besides, I didn't know how to hang them, and I couldn't rely on Mason for much of anything.

Our backyards were tiny little postage stamps and only semi-private. There was a black, wooden head-high sort of half-fence at the end of all of the apartment yards, but instead of a divider between each, there was only a divider between every two, as if these one-story apartments had been connected or meant to connect at some point. The Baumgartners' yard and ours meshed together and, while the blue and yellow U of M blanket was spread out over on their side, I could still see everything from my vantage point. And I mean *everything.*

I watched her drizzle oil over the copper colored flesh of her belly, her hands kneading it into the sloping curve of her ribs and onto the generous swell of her breasts, brazenly bared to the sun. I stayed quiet, swallowing my breath, as her palms made slow, lazy circles over her nipples and then dipped gently into the hollow of her throat, her slender, buttery fingers stroking her neck down to her collarbone.

I heard her sigh and saw her hips shift as her hands moved downward once again, lingering on the fullness of her breasts. She was so beautiful I could barely breathe, her hair spilling like honey against the navy blue blanket, her limbs long and shapely. I bit my lip when she pinched her nipples, hearing her again, a soft cry.

I ducked when she sat up on her elbows, sliding her dark glasses down so she could peer around. It was nearly noon on a Monday, the late August sun high and bright, still hot although it was moving steadily toward autumn. The kids were back in school just this week, the neighborhood quieter than it had been all summer.

She glanced around and thought she was alone. She didn't see me watching from the window as she slid her slick hand down the flat, sloping surface of her belly, under the elastic band of her black bikini bottoms. At first, I thought she was going to take those off too, but when her hand moved under them, fully between her legs, I understood.

Breathless, I watched as she began to touch herself, occasionally glancing around, worried she might get caught, that someone might walk by. Our little one-story apartments backed up to a small, wooded area. The kids liked to play there, but today there were no calls of "You're it!" and no one fighting over the tire swing someone had hung from a tree.

We were alone, she and I, two women longing for something, looking to ease a sudden, throbbing ache. I should have just turned away and gone back to studying my Italian phrasing, which is what I'd been doing before I heard the sound of her back door opening and closing, that tell-tale squeak and bang. But, as my mother would also attest, I rarely did the things I should do in life. Instead, I usually did the things people told me I shouldn't, and more importantly, I did the things I wanted to do.

And I wanted to watch. I was wearing jeans, too confining, but they were quickly unbuttoned and unzipped. I sought my own heat, my pussy moist, still shaved smooth the way Mason liked it. God, how long had it been since he'd touched me? I shoved that dark thought away and turned my attention to the luminous visage of the woman writhing on the lawn next door, taking her own unabashed pleasure.

Her hand moved rhythmically under the stretched crotch of her bikini bottoms, her face turned toward me. The dark sunglasses she wore kept her eyes from me, but I saw the part of her lips, the way the pink tip of her tongue slipped out and licked them. Her chest moved with her increasing breath, her breasts rising and falling, faster and faster.

My clit hid, untouched for so long, in the swollen folds of my flesh, but I managed to find it, shuddering at my body's response, as if I had an instant "on" switch I'd just rediscovered. I teased it to life, back and forth, round and round, my own breath coming faster, my nipples hard under my t-shirt as I pressed close to the wall, straining to see out the window.

The blond on the blanket flicked and tugged at her own nipples. They were brown and hard, like my own, although I was far paler than she and her breasts were a little bigger. We were both pretty well-endowed in that department though, and I cupped my breast though my bra with my other hand as if to check, rubbing my thumb over the ridge of my nipple, feeling the weight of it, wondering what her breast would feel like in my hand—heavy, oily, fleshy.

It wouldn't have been the first time I'd been with a woman. Before Mason, I'd been with Dee. My mother had insisted I was "going through a phase," and when Dee and I broke up in the midst of a huge drama over—what else?—some guy, my mother had crowed that I'd proven her right, that I wasn't a lesbian after all. I didn't know what I was—I just knew that women turned me on and men turned me on, and maybe aliens would turn me on, too, but I'd never met one. Maybe I was just greedy, insatiable. I had always wanted more than the world could ever give me. At least, I used to.

"Ohhhh!" The soft cry that rose up from her throat drew my attention back to the spectacle next door. She bit her lip, her tanned thighs spread and shining with oil, glistening in the sunlight. I wished then that she had taken her bottoms off too so I could watch her fingers plunging into her pussy, as fast and furious as my own, wishing for a cock, a tongue, something, everything at once.

I arched my back and rocked up and down, back and forth, riding my own hand, my nipples rubbing hard against the windowsill, forgetting myself, forgetting that I was supposed to stay quiet, unnoticed. I pressed my nose to the screen, catching the scent of fresh cut grass and coconut oil, imagining I could smell her too, the pungent aroma of her pussy. Was she shaved, like me? Was she blond down there or dark, I wondered? Just thinking about it was so exciting I had to slow down or I was going to climax right that second. And I wanted to wait.

I wanted to come with her.

"Oh! Oh! Oh!" She gasped and gave three short, sharp cries, her hips thrusting upward, her thighs butterflied wide, one hand rubbing herself frantically, the other clutching her breast, tweaking her nipple. The sight of her was enthralling, but it was the low, throaty growl she finally gave and the way her head thrashed from side to side as she came that finally sent me soaring.

I didn't just fall, I leapt, moaning and thrusting and diving headlong into the precipice, that same delicious edge I'd been flirting with and yet paradoxically trying to avoid since the moment I unzipped my jeans. I came so hard I couldn't see, couldn't hear, couldn't breathe, couldn't think. I didn't let myself go—there was no choice involved—I simply went, plunging headlong into bliss.

And that's when the screen fell out of the window. I'd been pressing on it so hard, it was no wonder. The springs that held it in just gave way and, if I hadn't caught myself, I would have fallen too. It wasn't a high fall, but it would have been an embarrassing one, considering that my hand was still plunged into the front of my unzipped jeans. It was embarrassing enough as it was as Carrie scrambled to grab her bikini top, tying it quickly on, and I zipped and tucked and yelled out some sort of apology across the yard.

It was Jezebel who gave me an excuse. I used her wanton lust to defend my own, claiming it was our cat that had knocked out the screen. She'd been sitting quietly next to me on the sill the whole while, occasionally licking a fat, black paw and rubbing it over one velvety ear, the only other witness to our sin. Jezebel looked askance at me when I offered her up as a sacrifice, her expression even more indignant than usual.

"It should just pop right back in." The blond walked across her yard and into mine, bending down to pick up the screen. "I've knocked ours out a couple times."

"Thanks." I took it awkwardly, shoving the sheet-curtain aside as I brought it through the window and dropped it next to the bed. As the screen passed between us, our hands touched—hers sleek and smelling of coconut and mine still wet with my juices, although I'd hastily wiped my hand on my jeans—and she smiled. "Sorry, I didn't mean to disturb you."

"I was just working on my tan." She glanced over to the blanket she'd been touching herself on and then looked back at me. Did she know I'd been watching? "Want to join me?"

"I—" I searched for some excuse. I didn't want to embarrass myself any further. "I don't own a bikini."

"You can borrow one of mine, if you want. I was only wearing half of one anyway." She grinned, adjusting her bikini top. She didn't even flush—but I did. "I'm Carrie Baumgartner, by the way. Nice to meet you, neighbor."

"Danielle Stuart," I replied. "They call me Dani."

"Come on, Dani." She waved me out, as if the decision had already been made. "Let's get some sun together."

And that was how it began.

Chapter One

We spent a week in our backyard—and I thought of it as "ours" by then, connected as it was—soaking up the last of the summer sun, Carrie in a black bikini and me wearing a modest one-piece, red with little white polka dots. I wasn't there for the sun and I think she knew it, although we spent that first week chatting about our husbands, campus life and our families—or lack thereof. Carrie had moved around from foster home to foster home as a kid, and hadn't had anything like a "real" family until she married Doc ("His name's Steve, but everyone calls him 'Doc,' even me," Carrie said) who I had yet to meet. That was another thing we had in common—husbands who were hardly ever home, although for vastly different reasons.

"He works so hard." Carrie sighed, turning her face to me on the blanket. She was on her belly, top undone, her hair curling at the edges with oil. No matter how much I showered that week, I went to bed smelling like coconuts and I inevitably dreamed of Carrie Baumgartner's tanned flesh. I was more than halfway crushing on her already. "You have to respect a man who loves what he does for a living. But I do miss him."

I nodded sympathetically. "I know what you mean." And I did, although missing Mason didn't leave me with stars in my eyes like missing Doc did for her. While her husband was doing his residency at the University of Michigan teaching hospital, mine was... well, I wasn't quite sure what he was doing most of the time. Hanging out in basements with his friends, rolling many-sided dice and conjuring spirits, most likely. It sounded too ridiculous to mention, even if we were four years younger than they were, so I just kept my mouth shut.

"Where did the sun go?" She craned her slim neck to see the sky, giving me a dizzying view of her cleavage. I could see the dark flower of her areolas and could almost glimpse their center. "Is it going to rain?"

"It better not rain on our last week of sunshine." I screwed up my face and stuck my middle finger up at the darkening clouds. "Classes start Monday."

"Oh that's right, I almost forgot." She turned her face back, rubbing her cheek against the blanket. Carrie had her undergraduate degree in something, but she hadn't decided to go back for a graduate degree, so she was taking occasional classes while Doc finished up his residency. Me, I was kind of excited for classes to begin again—it would be my last year. Besides, my major was my passion and I missed not being immersed several hours a day in classrooms where only Italian was spoken.

A loud clap of thunder shook the ground beneath us and both our heads came up, eyes widening as our gaze met.

"Uh oh." That was all I managed to get out before the skies opened and rained down on us. We both squealed, scrabbling for the blanket and our clothes. The t-shirt and shorts in my hands were already damp just in the time it took us to get to the Baumgartners' back door. Carrie pressed me inside, still topless, and pulled the screen door shut behind us. Lightning struck a tree in the woods and we both screamed and clutched each other, seeing the brief spark of a flame and then smoke. It was pouring, the splash of the rainwater wetting our faces through the screen.

"That was fast!" She closed the door as I moved fully into their kitchen. The apartment was the same layout as ours was, as they all were, the kitchen making the short part of an "L" that turned the corner into a living room. There was a bedroom off the kitchen, and I glanced in to confirm that, yes, there was a queen sized bed in there. Carrie and Doc's bedroom. Another door beyond that was closed—the second bedroom. We had one, too.

"I need a shower." Carrie slipped past me into her bedroom, turning on a light. It was like night outside now, the rain pelting the roof. I hesitated in the doorway. I'd never been in their apartment before. We always met in the yard. She hooked her thumbs in her bikini bottoms, glancing back at me as she slid them down her hips. There was no guile or self-consciousness in her look, but watching her made my mouth go dry. "You want to take a shower?"

I just nodded, not trusting my voice, and followed her as she walked naked toward the bathroom. Just like our apartment, the bathroom was attached to the first bedroom. Anyone who wanted to use it had to go through, which always made me uncomfortable when we had guests. Whoever designed the place obviously didn't have my anxiety about unmade beds. Carrie's was made though, spotless, the comforter a lovely patchwork thing, pulled taut, the shams to match on pillows against the headboard. I ran a finger over one of the seams, a zigzag stitch.

I heard the shower start and glanced at the open bathroom door. I could see her leaning over, breasts swaying, to adjust the water, her bottom round and full and shockingly pale compared to the rest of her.

"Nice tan lines," I commented and she made a face at me.

"If I didn't think one of the nosy neighbors would call the cops, I'd take my bottoms off too." She reached into the little closet and got out two big, fluffy light blue towels. They matched the shower curtain. I wasn't about to tell her that I had been one of those nosy neighbors just days ago. "I hate tan lines." She put the towels on the edge of the sink, glancing over at me. "Are you coming in? Don't be shy—we're both girls."

When she'd asked me if I wanted a shower, I'd sort of hoped but hadn't assumed that we'd be taking one together. Now that I was here, standing in the doorway of her bathroom with that question answered, I wasn't so sure. Especially since I had to take off my bathing suit to make it happen.

"Come on," she invited, turning fully toward me. "The water's warm."

Jesus, she was beautiful. I dropped my eyes, trying not to stare, and glimpsed the short, tight blond curls between her thighs for the first time. That sight gave me a jolt but when she slid her arms around my neck, untying my suit at the neck, I thought I might melt into the floor.

"Wait." I gulped as the top of my suit dropped to my waist, my breasts exposed to her view. I winced at the expression on her face when her gaze fell, her eyes widening.

"Oh my God." Her eyebrows drew together, her hand reaching out, hesitating, not touching. "What did you do?"

"I fell." I turned sideways and slid my suit down my hips. She'd seen now—there was no sense being modest anymore. Most of the bruises had faded, looking more like a Canadian sunrise across my middle instead of the storm clouds they had been a few days ago.

"You fell?" Her expression was doubtful. "Where? Off a roof?"

"I tripped over a chair in the kitchen, fell against the counter." I'd prepared this speech all week, just in case. And it wasn't entirely untrue. Not entirely. I made it sound casual, dismissive. "It doesn't hurt." I stepped into the shower to avoid the look in her eyes, the water hot, stinging my face. It was just a moment before I felt her get in behind me. I edged forward so I wasn't hogging all the spray.

"I have to tell you something." Carrie took the soap out of the dish, rubbing it thoughtfully in her hands, making suds. "But I don't want to make you mad at me."

"Why would I be mad?" I turned to look at her. We were almost the same height and we stood eye to eye, practically nose to nose, the steam rising around us. "You're the first friend I've had..." I blinked, glad for the water running down my cheeks. "In a long time."

"And friends should be able to tell each other things," she said, rubbing her soapy hands over her oil-slick shoulders. "Right?"

"Right," I agreed, although I wasn't quite sure what I was agreeing to.

"Well, then." She reached for the shampoo, giving up on the soap and slipping it back into the dish. "You have to know these walls are pretty thin." She nodded toward the tiles and squeezed shampoo into her cupped hand. "I'm sure you've heard us."

I flushed, glad for the heat of the shower turning my skin pink. "Sometimes." It was true that they might as well have used tissue paper to insulate the walls. I'd heard the two of them at night a few times, her sharp cries, his groans—and their bedroom was two rooms away from my own. Either they were incredibly loud or the walls were incredibly thin. Or a little of both.

"So tell me..." She worked the shampoo into her hair. "Do those bruises have anything to do with the yelling I heard coming from your place last week?"

"No." I denied it immediately, my arms crossed over my middle. "I fell."

She turned her back to me, letting the spray rinse the soap from her hair, working it out with her fingers. I took the soap and quickly washed, the smell of coconut strong in the moist heat. When she handed me the shampoo, I took it, using it as an excuse to close my eyes and turn away from her.

"I knew it would make you mad," she said in a small voice. I felt her fingertips brush over my shoulder, like bird's wings. "I'm sorry."

"I'm not mad." I shrugged. It was true—I wasn't mad. I was afraid. And I didn't want to talk about it. "Really, I'm not."

"So we're still friends?" she asked as I turned to face her.

"Friends who take showers together, apparently." I grinned.

"Nothing wrong with that." She laughed. "Can I ask you something else?"

I groaned. "Do you have to?"

"I was just wondering..." Her gaze fell briefly and then skipped back up again to meet mine. "Have you always shaved down there?"

I blinked and then glanced down too, as if to confirm what I already knew. "Well... not always. But Mason likes me smooth."

"Does he?" She cocked her head, looking again between my legs as if my response gave her permission. There was no hair there at all anymore. I used to have a dark little landing strip but Mason had made fun of me, saying it looked like my pussy had a Mohawk, so I'd gotten rid of it. "What's it like?"

"Haven't you ever gone bare?" I raised my eyebrows, looking down at her little nest of curls. She was definitely a real blond. "You, with your penchant for bikinis?"

"Well, I keep it trimmed." Her hand went there, her fingers pulling gently at her pubic hair. It reminded me of seeing her touching herself from my bedroom window and the memory made my knees weak.

"You could wear one of those little micro-bikinis if you shaved," I pointed out. "Less tan lines. And I bet your husband would love it."

"You think?" Her eyes brightened at the thought.

"Sure. It makes things easier. Less in the way." I waggled my eyebrows and she grinned. I leaned in, lowering my voice, as if I might be overheard. "The first time I did it, I couldn't believe how sensitive I was down there afterward."

"Really?" she breathed. We'd been drinking sun tea and her breath smelled minty against my cheek. "I'd be afraid, though. What if I cut myself?" She shuddered.

"It takes practice." I nodded sagely, the idea coming out of my mouth before I could even think. "I could help you. Show you how I do it."

"On you?" She licked her lips, her gaze dipping again to my bare mound.

"Or on you." I pointed between her thighs, where her hand was still idly stroking the hair there. "If you really want to."

"Okay." She grabbed my wrist, squeezing. "Let's do it." She was so excited she was practically vibrating. "What do we need?"

"Just a good razor and some shaving cream."

She was out of the shower before I could finish my sentence, opening the medicine cabinet, taking a disposable razor out of its plastic and handing me a red and white striped can. She shoved them both at me. "Here. Where do you want me?"

I glanced around the bathroom. I usually shaved in the shower, putting one leg up on the edge. Would that work, if I knelt in the tub? I wondered.

"Here." I opened the curtain wider so she could step in. She was shivering, her nipples stiff, the skin around them pursed. She hesitated, looking a little afraid, and I smiled. "It doesn't hurt. I promise. I'll be gentle."

"How?" She looked around, frowning, as I sank to my knees, the hot water needling my back.

"Put your foot up in the corner and sort of lean back." I guided her with my words, not daring yet to touch her. My hands were shaking and that wasn't the best state in which to be handling a razor.

"Like this?" She did as I directed, her palm resting against her lower belly, peering down at the soft fuzz between her legs.

"Perfect," I said, and she was. Her thighs were long, tawny muscled velvet and I couldn't help placing my palm there, as if to steady myself, just to feel the incredible softness of her. "Are you ready?"

I glanced up and saw her bite her lip, her breasts beaded with water, rising and falling with her breath. Her hair turned darker when wet, less honey and more wheat, some of it making little curls against her cheeks and her neck. Seeing her like that, her thighs parted, her eyes wide with excitement and even a little fear, made my mouth water.

"Do it," she insisted, closing her eyes tight and looking the other way. It gave me the opportunity to really study her and I smiled, squirting shaving cream into my hand. Her pussy was truly lovely and I almost hated to shave off her blond curls. She flinched a little and opened one eye when I started to spread the shaving cream over her bush.

"It's okay," I soothed. She closed her eyes again, looking away. She kept it trimmed with scissors, so the hair wasn't too long to begin with. I made short, easy strokes downward. "All of it?" I inquired, hesitating as I reached the middle of the triangle.

Again, she opened just one eye. "Yeah. Let's go for it."

"All right." I rinsed the blade in the inch or so of water gathered at the bottom of the tub, continuing the job. I had most of the long hairs gone on her labia, but there was much more intimate work to be done. I glanced up at her turned face, her eyes still scrunched closed, and then used my fingers to delicately part her pussy lips.

"Ohhh." She barely breathed the word, biting her lip as my fingers brushed her clit. It was difficult to keep her open and manipulate the razor at the same time. She wasn't just wet from the shower—she was slippery. Aroused. God knows I was too. My pussy felt fat and swollen, and I squeezed my thighs together, resisting the urge to touch myself as I used the razor, making upward strokes now.

"Almost done," I assured her, using my fingers to feel for stray hairs and any stubble I might have missed. Her skin was like silk, her juices making her pussy slick. Her lips were swollen and I petted her gently, hearing her sigh softly as I neared the top of her cleft, feeling the slight forward shift of her hips. I wondered if she could feel my breath on her thigh, coming faster now. I couldn't help it.

"Oh God," she whispered, her thigh quivering under my palm as I steadied her, continuing with my inspection. Her eyes were closed to just slits as she looked down at me. "It's sooo sensitive now."

"I told you." I smiled smugly, sitting back on my heels. "I think we're done."

"Really?" She opened her eyes fully, sliding a hand down to touch herself. I watched, transfixed, as her fingers explored the soft, completely nude folds of her own flesh for the first time. "Oh wow. It's so different. So *smooth*."

I had to stand up. If I didn't, I was going to do something crazy. It was hard enough, pretending I wasn't aroused by her, not knowing if she wanted more, afraid to ask. She was so unselfconscious, so open with her body, I still wasn't sure, and I didn't want to risk the newness of our friendship because I couldn't control my urges. Funny, that. I hadn't had any urges for so long, and now I had one so strong I was finding it almost impossible to resist it.

"He's going to be so surprised!" She gasped, her fingers still exploring, giving me a delighted smile. "Oh Dani, thank you so much!"

She threw her arms around my neck and hugged me, the soft, wet press of her breasts against mine a brief, delightfully yielding moment of heaven. She laughed as she drew back, looking down and tilting her hips toward mine. "Look, now we match. We're like twins."

That made me laugh too and we got out of the shower together to dry off. Carrie got dressed in shorts and a t-shirt and I put mine on too, although I didn't have panties or a bra. I considered running next door for them, but Carrie insisted I stay and eat with her. She'd been cooking something all day in a crockpot. I could smell it simmering. Besides, it was still pouring outside, the sky even darker.

"White chicken chili," she announced. "Doc loves it. It's supposed to be for dinner, but I'm hungry now."

"Perfect for a rainy day." I looked around for a place where we might eat our lunch. Our kitchens were far too small for tables. There was a small area in the living room that we used as a dining area where I had a table, but the Baumgartners had a desk and computer there.

"Stupid rain." Carrie made a face as she glanced out the window. "I wish we lived in Florida."

"Too many big bugs." I shuddered. "How about Rome? It's nice and sunny there."

"I don't know any Italian."

"But I do." I smiled.

"Okay, you take me to Italy and we'll take you to Florida." She opened the crockpot and stirred. "We're going to Florida for Christmas."

"That sounds like fun." I looked over her shoulder. It smelled delicious.

"Doc's parents have a timeshare there. There's a private beach. We can just walk out and go swimming in the ocean." She took out a bowl and started spooning chili into it. She handed me the bowl and reached into the cupboard for another. Then she turned to me, a funny expression on her face. "Wow, you weren't kidding. It feels like I'm going around naked or something."

I smiled. "Yeah, I know." I couldn't help imagining her panties hugging her pussy, the seam of her shorts rubbing into her slit every time she moved, no hair there to impede them.

We spent all afternoon watching movies and complaining about the rain. It never did let up. The parking lot flooded. It was hard to tell what time it really was because it was so dark. The streetlights had been on for hours.

"Let's pretend it's Venice," Carrie joked, coming up behind me at the window. I felt her breath on my neck and it made me shiver.

The door opened, surprising us both, and a very wet, dark haired man came in, shutting the rain out behind him. "It's crazy out there! I think I saw an ark parked down the street."

That made me laugh and Carrie ran to him, putting her arms around his neck. "You're early! You weren't supposed to be home until midnight!"

He glanced at his watch, still shaking off the rain. "It's almost ten. Okay, so I slipped out a little early. I missed you, what can I say?" He glanced over at me. "Is this the Dani I've heard about all week?"

Carrie beamed happily. "Dani, this is Doc."

"Nice to meet you." It sounded so strange and formal, but he just smiled.

"I'm soaked through. I'm gonna take a shower. Is that white chicken chili I smell? You are a goddess!" He kissed his wife on the cheek and headed toward the bedroom. She stood there for a moment, looking after him, and then back at me.

"I should go home," I said, moving slowly toward the door. "It's getting late."

"Don't you dare!" Doc called. "I brought home margarita mix and we've got a ton of ice!"

Carrie grinned. "Want to stay and get drunk?"

I hardly ever drank but that didn't matter. She didn't have to ask me twice. "Absolutely."

Doc ate his chili and exclaimed over it the whole time. I had to admit, it was pretty fantastic. Then he started making margaritas and Carrie put "Ghost" into the VCR.

"Again?" Doc complained good-naturedly. "Ever since it won the Academy Award, she can't get enough of it."

"Oh shut up." She stuck her tongue out at him. "You want Demi Moore and you know it. Besides, the pottery scene is *hot.*"

"I wouldn't say no if she wanted to eat crackers in my bed." Doc cocked his head at me, refilling my margarita. "You look a little like her. Longer hair, of course."

I smiled, sipping my drink. "I actually get that a lot."

We settled on the couch. I expected Carrie to cuddle with Doc, but instead she insisted I sit between them. I thought it would be strange, that I would feel out of place, but things fit so well, as if we were puzzle pieces finding their niche. Doc poked fun at the movie and Carrie teased him and I couldn't get over how easy and comfortable it felt. It could have been the alcohol loosening me up, but I was sure that wasn't all of it.

Doc slipped an arm around my shoulder and I didn't protest. Carrie leaned her head against me and rubbed her cheek absently against Doc's hand while we watched. Doc kept refilling our margaritas—I lost count of how many times he went back out to the kitchen to refill the blender with ice—and that feeling of being warm and comfortable turned into sleepiness after a while.

I made it through the pottery scene—which was decidedly hot and made me squirm, feeling Carrie's bare thigh against mine, and Doc's jean-clad one rubbing against the other—but I dozed off at some point after Whoopi Goldberg tried to convince Demi Moore that Patrick Swayze was trying to communicate with her from the other side. When I woke, Carrie was covering me with a blanket, the TV was off and the room was dark.

"I have to go home," I murmured, trying to sit. Bad idea. The room spun. Way too many margaritas for me.

"Shhh." She tucked the blanket under my chin. "You sleep. I'm going to show Doc our little... *surprise.*"

It took my foggy brain a few moments to realize what she was talking about, but by then she had gone to her room. My thoughts lingered on her, reliving the silky slickness of her pussy against my fingers as I shaved her. He was definitely going to be surprised, I thought, and found myself feeling jealous. Then I recalled her words, "*our* little surprise." Somehow she had included me in it and that was gratifying. I let the alcohol win again and slept.

Something woke me. I'd been sleeping hard, drooling on the edge of the couch cushion, my arm dangling off the edge, dreaming about Patrick Swayze making margaritas, and something pulled me suddenly from sleep. I had no idea what it was—I couldn't hear anything but the rain, still falling, and the ticking of a clock somewhere—and then I didn't care. I was suddenly desperate to pee. All those damned margaritas. I pulled myself to standing, using the back of the couch to steady myself in the unfamiliar darkness. My head was still spinning. I hardly ever drank anymore, even wine.

It was nearly dark, but there was a night light in the kitchen next to the sink and I followed its glow, shuffling along the carpet in my bare feet. The last thing I wanted to do was trip and wake the Baumgartners. It wasn't until I'd made my way through the kitchen and saw the bedroom door, slightly ajar, that I remembered the way to the bathroom was through their room.

Then I heard an unmistakable moan and knew what had woken me. They were having sex. What I'd mistaken for a ticking clock was the rhythmic tap of a headboard hitting the wall.

"Oh God, that's fucking fantastic!" Carrie gasped. "I'm going to come again!"

I heard him grunt, the springs squeaking louder, faster, the headboard slapping the wall with greater force. She gave three short, sharp cries, the same sound I'd heard her make that afternoon watching from the window, and I felt my whole body bloom with warmth. I leaned against the door frame for support, not sure I could trust my legs to keep me up.

"I love your shaved little pussy," he growled. The squeaking had stopped. "Gimme!"

"No, no, no!" she cried. There was a flurry and shuffle and she objected the whole while but then I heard her moan softly. "Oh God, Doc, I can't, not again..."

"Mmmm yes you can," he assured her, his words muffled. I was sure his mouth was full. I felt so faint I thought I might actually pass out. "God, that's so fucking hot. So *smooth.*"

"I *know.*" She sounded both smug and proud. "She shaved me so nice."

"She sure did." More muffled words from Doc.

"Oh baby, your tongue!"

I'd obviously guessed correctly.

"So tell me about your shower." Doc's voice was low. "Did you enjoy it?"

"You're bad." She teased him. "Does it turn you on, thinking about the two of us wet and naked?"

"You know it does." His grin was so big I could hear it in his voice. "Tell me."

"She's so pretty, Doc," she murmured dreamily. "Her breasts are big like mine, but she's got these puffy nipples, so sexy."

He groaned. "What color?"

"Brown, almost as dark as mine," she murmured. I couldn't believe the details she was relaying, how much she had noticed about me. That confirmed she'd been looking too, maybe as much as I had. I cupped my breast in my hand, closing my eyes, imagining the weight of hers, seeing the fat pursed jut of her nipples in my mind. I thumbed my own nipple through my shirt and shivered. "And her pussy, oh God, she's shaved so smooth. I wanted to touch it... and kiss it."

Me, too, I thought, and squeezed my legs together, feeling the heightened pulse between them. I'd been imagining little else for a week, and knowing now that she'd been thinking about it too made me so hungry for her, my mouth actually started to water.

"More," Doc insisted, his breath coming fast. "Tell me more."

"I want your cock first." She made a little sound, denying him. "No, no, not there—in my mouth."

He hesitated. "Then you can't tell me."

"My hand then," she conceded and I heard them rearranging on the bed. I wished I could see but the room was dark. Maybe if I pushed the door open a little further? I chanced it, praying it didn't squeak, opening it just another inch.

"Oh God. Easy." Doc gasped. "I haven't come yet."

"You're going to," she purred.

"Not yet," he pleaded. I could see their outlines, ghosts and shadows. She was on top of him, her hand wrapped around his cock, her pussy poised over his face.

"Did she touch you?" He urged her on.

"She had to," Carrie replied with a little snort of laughter. "She shaved my pussy, remember?"

"No, I mean, did she *touch* you."

"I think so." She sounded thoughtful and the motion of her hand slowed. "She brushed my clit more than once and I don't think it was all by accident."

They were quiet for a moment and I strained to hear, wishing I had Jezebel's ability to see perfectly well in the dark. I wanted to see his cock. I wanted to watch her stroke him. I really wanted to see her arched above him, moving her hips against his tongue. What I really wanted was to be sandwiched somewhere in the midst of all that sweaty, wanton flesh. My pussy felt swollen, hot.

"Why didn't you take her to bed with you?" Doc asked. "Didn't you want to?"

"Oh God yes..." Her reply was breathy, dreamy. "It just feels so funny, without you..."

He snorted. "You have my permission."

"I know."

They stopped talking, concentrating on other things. There was just the sound of their breath and their bodies rocking, rubbing, licking. Oh God, I was so wet. I had to touch myself. I had to.

"Do it," Doc insisted, and at first I thought he was talking to me. I froze, breath caught, eyes wide, my hand sneaking under the waistband of my shorts. Then I realized he was talking to her.

"Oh Doc," Carrie murmured.

"Do it for me," he urged her. "So you can tell me all about it."

He was telling her to do it—to do *me*. And I wanted her to. Oh yes, I did. I cupped my aching mound, my labia puffy and wet.

"I'd love to taste her," Carrie admitted, her voice lowered, as if she was telling him a secret.

"So soft and smooth," he said, inciting her lust even more. "Just like your little pussy now."

"I want to rub our pussies together," she whispered hoarsely. "Make them kiss."

He groaned like a man being tortured. "Do you think she wants to?"

"She wants to." She was quite confident. And she was right. "And you know what?"

"Hmm?" He sounded distracted, busy, and I imagined his face buried between her sweet, tanned thighs, arms wrapped around her hips, her pussy spread wide for his tongue. My clit came to life the moment my fingers found it, slippery wet and thrumming with excitement.

"After tonight, I think she might want you too," she hinted.

He groaned. "You know I wouldn't say no to that."

The thought made my pussy hum. I couldn't deny that it had occurred to me, sitting there tonight, lodged between them on the couch. He was sexy as hell, and the two of them together? Oh God, what was I thinking? I was married. *They* were married. And somehow none of that mattered.

"But if she doesn't want me, that's okay," Doc was saying and I almost cried out in protest. Instead I bit my lip, my fingers moving faster over my tingling little clit, teasing it toward climax. I wanted it so badly my thighs quivered. "You two can still have fun. I want you to."

Carrie sighed happily. "You are the most amazing man in the world." I couldn't have agreed more. Then she said, "I want your cock in me. Fuck me."

He chuckled. "Not until you come in my mouth."

"Oh God," she whimpered. "I don't think I can."

"Oh yes you can," he contended. "Just imagine her sitting on your face." She moaned and thrashed on the bed. My fingers circled my clit, zeroing in, chasing my orgasm, wishing it was Carrie's tongue, that I really was sitting on her face. That she was on mine. Oh God, how I wanted it. Doc was still talking—talking and licking, licking and urging her on. Urging me on too.

"Grinding her pussy against your tongue. Yeah, just like that. Oh baby, your cunt tastes so fucking good."

"Eat it!" she hissed, sounding more out of control than I'd ever heard her. "Oh yes, I want her pussy so bad. I can almost taste her."

"Taste," he growled and I heard a wet, sucking sound. She was licking her juices off his fingers, I just knew it. I wanted to taste, too. Instead, I shoved another hand down my shorts, scooping my fingers through my slit, gathering a bit of slippery wetness and bringing it to my mouth. I rubbed the slickness over my lips, sucking at my fingers, never stopping the desperate circles against my clit.

"Come for me!" he persisted. *Oh fuck.* Yes, I was going to. I was going to come for him, for her, for them. "Come all over my face!"

My bladder was so full I thought if I climaxed I just might pee myself, but I didn't care. I rubbed myself furiously, panting, listening, imagining.

"Oh Doc! Oh! Oh! Oh!" It was the sound of her that did it for me, Carrie coming, hips thrusting, thighs straining. I could almost see her in the dark and my pelvis jutted forward too as if she was a magnet drawing me toward her.

Doc growled and the headboard hit the wall hard. Carrie howled. He was fucking her good, driving into her. I could hear them both panting, grunting, gasping in the darkness.

"I'm going to come!" he announced. "Ahhhh fuck, it's so good!"

"Come on, baby," she cried. "Come in my pussy. I want her to lick all your cum out of my cunt."

"Oh God."

That did it. For all of us, I think. She made those sweet cries again and Doc grunted and groaned. Me, I bit my lip and thanked God that the wall held me up because I had both hands shoved deep into my shorts, riding my orgasm like a tidal wave between my thighs. My chest heaved, my nipples so hard they hurt, and my panties and shorts were soaked with my cum.

And I still had to pee. Now more than ever.

"Shhhh." Carrie giggled. "She might hear us."

"She's probably listening right now, masturbating on the sofa."

"No way!" Carrie exclaimed and I froze, holding my breath. "You think so?"

"Want to go find out?"

"You're bad." She giggled again and I heard them rearranging again in the dark.

I crept away from the door as quietly as I could, finding my way back to the couch and collapsing there, pulling the blanket back over me. I could hardly catch my breath, but I still wanted more. My pussy insisted, and I did just what Doc said I would—I touched myself again on the sofa, reliving the moment, imagining them both, in me, on me, all over me. Finally sated, I drifted, my bladder complaining until sleep took me, but I didn't dare go through their room to the bathroom. Who knew what I might do?

Chapter Two

Morning dawned like a gift, sun streaming in the windows, the world washed clean. I woke up to Doc squatting next to the sofa holding a cup of hot coffee and smiling.

"Thought you might want this." He held it out and I groaned, opening both eyes and focusing. He was wearing a t-shirt and boxer shorts, his dark hair tousled from sleep. "Not much of a drinker, are you?"

"Not much," I acknowledged hoarsely, sitting up and reaching for the warm mug. My bladder rebelled immediately—*no more liquid input until we have output!* "Bathroom," I stated flatly, handing the mug back to him and scrambling up.

"Are you going to throw up?" he called sympathetically as I bolted toward the door.

"Pee!" I countered, rounding the corner, glancing briefly at their bed, still unmade. Carrie wasn't in it. The shower was running, but I opened the bathroom door anyway, making for the toilet. I'd never had to pee so badly in my life.

"Hey you." Carrie poked her head out to see me as I sighed in relief, finally relaxing and letting go. My kidneys actually hurt. "How'd you sleep?"

"Good." I felt my face redden and I pulled my t-shirt down a little, embarrassed, although God only knows why. I'd been in a shower with her yesterday, touching her privates and shaving her clean, and last night...

Well, she didn't know about last night, did she? That was my secret.

She ducked back into the shower, calling out, "That couch can be killer if you get in the wrong position."

"It was fine." I finished and flushed the toilet, turning the water on to wash my hands.

"Eiiieeee!" Carrie squealed and poked her head back out. "Don't flush!"

"Too late," I apologized, wincing. "I forgot, sorry." I knew how the water worked in these apartments. We couldn't do dishes and run a bath in the same hour or the hot water would run out, and the shower always turned freezing the moment anyone flushed. With Mason gone so much, I'd lost any sense of water temperature decorum.

"It's coming back." She sounded relieved. "Do you want to shower after me?"

"I have to go home." I glanced in the mirror. My hair was a dark messy cloud around my face and down my back, out of control. "I have to feed my cat."

"Do you want to do something later?" She stuck her head back out again, face beaded with water, hair wet and slicked back, making her blue eyes even more striking. "Doc's got to be back at the hospital by five."

"Sure." I didn't know why I felt shy now when I'd been so comfortable before. "Last night was fun."

"We should do it more often." She winked and pulled the curtain again.

"Talk to you later?" I called.

"Definitely!"

I made my way back through the kitchen and found Doc sitting on the sofa in the living room with a newspaper, a TV tray set up with two mugs sitting on it. He looked up and smiled when he saw me hesitating the in the doorway.

"Here's your coffee." He nodded toward the table. "Want to join me?"

I should have declined, for a myriad of reasons, but I didn't. Instead I took a seat on the couch opposite him.

"Which section do you want?" he asked, shuffling through the paper.

"International."

He raised an eyebrow, flipping through and pulling out that section of the paper for me. "Hm, that's different. Carrie always asks for entertainment first."

"My husband reads the comics first." I looked at the paper just to have something to do. The news was too depressing for me anymore. I didn't watch or read it. I couldn't stand to.

"Let me guess," I mused. "You read sports first."

"Politics." He winked. "And health and medicine, of course. But I won't deny checking the NHL standings occasionally."

I sipped my coffee, surprised at the flavor. "This is really good."

"Gourmet coffee. One of my indulgences." He smiled sheepishly. "Kona's a Hawaiian company. A little bit of tropical heaven in a cup."

"You guys like warm places," I observed. "Carrie was telling me about the timeshare in Florida."

He nodded. "My parents' place. Yeah, my girl loves the sun. Looks like you've got quite a head start on her in that department, though." His gaze moved down over my thighs, lingering there. I'd only been hanging out with Carrie for a week and I was already darker than she was.

"I just have that olive sort of skin that tans fast." I felt my cheeks flush at the intensity of his stare.

"It's lovely." He sipped his coffee, our eyes meeting over the rim of the mug. He had dark eyes and the way he looked at me made me wonder what he was thinking.

"Thank you." I put my coffee back on the TV tray.

"Well, I should get home. My husband..." How to finish that sentence? He wasn't waiting for me. He hadn't been home since Carrie had heard us fighting, and that had been a bad one. The worst yet.

"We should all get together some time," Doc suggested.

"Thanks for the coffee," I said, changing the subject as I headed toward the door.

"Carrie really likes you," he said. I stopped, my hand on the doorknob, to look back at him. "I just wanted you to know. She's had a hard time here, since we moved from Boston, finding people to connect with. I'm glad you're friends."

I softened at his words. "I'm glad too."

My front door was locked. I'd gone out the back into the yard to sunbathe with Carrie and had forgotten to bring my keys. If I hadn't gone all the way around back, I wouldn't have known Mason was home until I got inside. His moped was parked in our yard, chained to the fence. It was the fastest way to get around campus and his parents had bought him one last Christmas. Only the best for their boy. My heart leapt when I saw it.

I went through the back door into the kitchen, closing it quietly behind me. Jezebel came over to greet me with a quizzical "mew," asking where I'd been all night. I noticed a can of food opened for her on the floor. He hadn't bothered putting it in her dish and he'd left the lid half-on, the edge sharp, but at least he'd fed her.

"Here, precious." I picked up the can. Miss Picky had only eaten half of it. I turned the rest into her bowl, tossing the can into the garbage. Her tail rose immediately and she settled herself in front of her dish as if to say, "This is more like it."

I took a deep breath and opened our bedroom door. The screen was still propped against the wall—it had been a week and I still hadn't managed to figure out how to put it back—but at least I'd remembered to shut the window before I left.

"Mace," I whispered. He was on his back in bed, snoring gently, an arm thrown across his eyes against the light. The sheet didn't do much to keep out the sun and it was getting bright. I hesitated, part of me desperate to climb in with him, another part of me heeding the "warning" sign flashing in my head. I went past, into the bathroom, turning on the shower. I stood under the hot water for a long time, until it started turning cool, before getting out and toweling off.

"Dani?" His voice was sleepy, eyes still closed as I opened the door.

It was warm and stuffy—we didn't have air conditioning—especially with the steam of the shower seeping into our bedroom, and Mason had just the sheet tangled around his waist. He was a beautiful man, his arms defined, chest broad. He'd cut his sandy brown hair, buzzed it short for the summer, and I fought the urge to get into bed with him and run my hand over his shorn head.

"Where were you last night?" he asked.

I snugged the towel around me tighter, just looking at him. "I could ask you the same thing."

He sighed. "I don't want to fight."

"I don't either," I replied in a small voice, remembering our last fight with painful clarity, but I relented when he opened his eyes and held a hand out to me. I went to him in spite of myself, dropping my towel and slipping under the covers beside him.

"Your hair's wet." He kissed the top of my head as I tucked it under his chin, resting my cheek against his chest, a heartbreakingly familiar position. His arms were strong and warm and I let him hold me for the first time in a very long while, closing my eyes and drifting.

When his hand moved under the covers, sliding up over my hip, fitting my body more fully against his and sliding a thigh between mine, I welcomed his intimate heat and weight. I let him kiss me, his tongue probing, letting myself go soft and open beneath him as we rolled, our bodies joining in silent apology to one another.

I was still wet from last night, from touching myself and listening, and the memory served as kindling to our fire. I was desperate for him, something in me awakened, brought to life again, a Frankenstein's monster charged with energy, reborn and hungry.

"Dani!" He gasped in surprise at my wild response, probably shocked that I was responding at all. I had been a rigid sheet of ice in my own corner of the bed for months after Isabella was gone. Then he had left the permafrost of our marriage for warmer climes, a catalyst that had allowed me to finally melt into a flood of tears.

He was hard and thick in my hand, thrusting in spite of himself. I saw the doubt in his eyes. I saw it and felt it and pushed past it, squeezing and rubbing him up and down against my slit, teasing us both. We both hesitated, breathing hard already with the gravity and weight of the moment. This was the act that had begun and ended our whole life together.

"Are you sure?" He nuzzled my neck, sucking at my skin, my wet hair. No, I wasn't sure. I wasn't sure of anything anymore. The world had turned upside down and I was walking on the ceiling all the time now, always afraid of falling.

My only response was to slide him into me, opening my thighs and letting him thrust, taking him deep. I hid my face against his chest, wrapping myself around him, arms and legs, so he wouldn't see me welling up with tears. It was the first time anything, anyone, had touched me inside since Isabella.

"Oh Dani," he whispered, taking everything I had to give him, his breath hot against my hair. "Oh you feel so good."

"So do you." I squeezed him hard, making him groan and thrust faster. I couldn't get enough and I shoved my pelvis up to meet his, again and again. For that moment, everything else disappeared and it was just us, as it had been. He was mine and I was the girl who loved him completely, without restraint or regret.

I panted and clung to him, digging my heels into the well of his back as if I could drive him in further, take him wholly into me. He moaned and slowed, gasping, "Wait, wait," in my ear, but I wouldn't let him go.

"Don't stop," I begged, my nails digging into his upper arms as he held himself over me. "Please! Don't stop!"

His eyes met mine, half-lidded with lust, his mouth slightly open. I whimpered and he dipped his head to kiss me, sucking my tongue into his mouth as he began again, his groan swallowed in the press and roll of our tongues. I planted my feet on the bed and lifted my hips, seeing his eyes roll back as he bottomed out inside of me.

"Harder!" I urged, my fingers seeking my own heat, searching between us for the place where we were joined, slick and hot and wet. I rubbed myself as he fucked me harder, giving me just what I'd asked for, although I knew it was going to cost him everything. His cock twitched inside of me and he rolled, pulling me on top of him and lifting me off the bed with one final thrust.

"Noooo," I howled, almost there but not quite, feeling him coming, knowing the look on his face, brow knitted, eyes closed tight, his lower lip pulled between his teeth.

"Fuck," he panted, reaching up and grabbing my breasts, thumbing my nipples. "I couldn't stop."

I whimpered, still rubbing myself, and he glanced down, his fingers tracing over my ribs, my belly.

I saw him cringe, seeing the bruises there. "Did I do that?"

"It doesn't matter." It did, but I didn't care, not then. I wanted him in spite of everything.

"I'm sorry," he whispered, his hands petting me from my breasts down to my pussy. "I'm so sorry."

"Mason," I pleaded, and he knew, he gave me just what I needed, he always had. I let him pull me up to his face, moaning softly when his mouth settled over my mound. It wasn't going to take much, but oh God, it felt so good I didn't ever want it to stop.

His tongue lapped at me, finding my clit right away, so sensitive and ready. I shuddered, spreading my legs wide and rocking. His hands on my hips moved to steady me and I stilled, letting him do all the work, my pussy on fire. There was no holding it back. I leaned my cheek against the wall behind us—we didn't have a headboard like the Baumgartners, we didn't even have a bed frame, just a boxspring and mattress on the floor—and gave in to my orgasm.

"Mason!" I gasped as his tongue fluttered at my clit, sending me flying. He moaned into my pussy as I came, flooding him with my juices, burying his face there for more as if he could drink me in altogether. My knees gave out and I collapsed next to him on the bed, laughing as he kissed me, his face still wet with my cum.

"Come here," he said, curling around me on the bed, pulling the covers up around us. We were quiet for quite a while and I thought he might be asleep until Jezebel jumped up onto the bed and climbed across Mason's hip and side, sniffing and twitching him with her whiskers as if to say, "Hello, stranger!"

"So, where were you last night?" he asked again, sliding a hand down Jezzie's back, making her arch. I blushed, watching them over my shoulder and remembering how he could make me do that, just like a cat.

"At the neighbors'." I flushed even more deeply at the memory of my night at the Baumgartners'. "It was raining so hard, they thought I should stay."

"I didn't know you hung out with the neighbors."

I snorted. "You don't know a lot of things that happen around here."

"Touché," he said softly, not taking the bait.

I turned toward him so we were belly to belly. "What brings you home?"

"Same thing that kept you at the neighbors, I guess." He stopped petting the cat and started petting me, his hand moving over my shoulder and down my side. "I was on my way back to Darron's and it was raining so damned hard I could barely see."

Darron the dungeonmaster. He had an apartment on the edge of campus and they played Dungeons and Dragons there three times a week. Mason and I had argued about how much time he spent there even before Isabella and now he was living in Darron's basement.

I couldn't help feeling disappointed. "So you didn't come home to see me?"

"No," he replied honestly. "But I'm glad I did."

That warmed me. "I'm glad too."

"Hey, I'm hungry," he said. "What do we have for breakfast?"

"I can make eggs." The fridge was pretty empty. I didn't have to do a lot of shopping with Mason gone. He was a big eater, but I could live on Lean Cuisines forever.

"That sounds good. Can I take a shower?" He slipped out of bed, stretching, and I admired the taut flex of the muscles in his back. I really had missed him, in so many ways.

"Go for it. You still have clothes in the closet." He'd never really moved out completely. He was doing it piecemeal, coming back and taking a few more things with him every time he left.

Mason ran the shower and I got dressed and cooked him eggs—four scrambled. I even made him toast with extra butter and cut them into fours. I was humming to myself, just putting the ketchup on the table, when he came out wearing a pair of jeans and nothing else.

"Thanks." He sat at the table across from me, squirting ketchup all over his eggs before digging in while I watched and nibbled my own slice of toast.

"How's Darron?" I didn't really want to know, but it was somewhere to start conversation.

"Good." His mouth was half-full. "We're thinking about starting a new thing that just came out. It's called *Magic the Gathering.*"

"Sounds cool." I had no idea what that meant. I'd never paid much attention to his gaming.

"Right." Mason snorted, giving me a look that said he knew just how much I cared—or not. "So, what classes you got this semester?"

"Advanced Italian, Dante's Divine Comedy, Senior Honors and Advanced Independent Study." I rattled them off—my last year's worth of work before graduation, all paid for by my scholarship. At least that was one thing Mason's parents didn't pay for. They'd paid for everything since we got married—our rent, our groceries, Mason's tuition—but my education was my own.

"Heavy load." He raised his eyebrows.

"So, what do you have this term?" It hurt me to think we were so disconnected now we didn't know these basic things.

He chewed his eggs and swallowed. "Survey of American Folklore and European History."

"Are you still majoring in sociology?"

"I switched to general studies."

The catch-all degree. He'd changed his major six times since we'd started school.

"Did you hear back from that study abroad thing?" He smiled when he picked up a triangle of toast and I knew he was appreciating that I'd remembered.

I stiffened and shook my head, busying myself with my own toast. The "study abroad thing" was my dream. I'd always wanted to go to Europe and, because of my scholarship, I'd been asked to apply to a very competitive program that would allow me to do all of my graduate work in Italy. The "study abroad thing" was also the topic of our last argument, the one that got me pushed into the kitchen table as Mason shoved by me on his way out the door. Needless to say, he didn't want me to go.

"You still set on doing that?" He popped a whole quarter triangle of toast into his mouth, chewing fiercely. I just nodded, not trusting my voice to answer him. "I can't go to Italy. My parents would have a fit. They'd never allow it."

Sure. They allowed him to skip school, fail classes and play D&D all day, but follow his wife to Italy so she could pursue her dreams? Oh no, never that.

"You're a big boy." I stood and took my empty plate to the sink. "Don't you think it's about time you started cutting some apron strings and making your own decisions?"

I held my breath. It was like déjà-vu. We were going to have the same argument all over again. Maybe this time he'd do more than just push me and bruise my ribs. Maybe this time he'd break an arm or my skull.

"It's not just them." He was on the defensive now. "I don't want to go to Italy. What am I going to do in *Italy?*"

"I don't know." I rinsed my plate, feeling Jezebel twining around my ankles. "What are you doing *here?*"

"I have no idea." He stood, the rest of his toast untouched. I closed my eyes as he started toward me and let out my pent-up breath when he passed, going into the bedroom. He came back out a few minutes later, fully dressed, while I was sitting quietly at the kitchen table and Jezebel licked up the remains of Mason's eggs.

He didn't even say goodbye when he grabbed his helmet from the table and took off out the back door. But I didn't call him back either. I just sat there and cried and wished, not for the first time or the last, that I had died instead of Isabella.

I was in the middle of reading Dante's Divine Comedy—in the original Italian, of course—just entering Purgatory and thinking about Mason and Isabella and the ruin my life had slowly become, when the phone rang.

"Oh my God, Dani, turn on the TV." It was Carrie. I glanced at the clock—it was almost eight at night and I remembered she said Doc started at the hospital at five.

I grabbed the remote, my stomach clenched. "What is it?" I flipped the TV on, sure something horrible had happened. Like I needed one more disaster?

"Turn to channel three-sixteen."

I frowned, pushing buttons on the remote. "Three-sixteen?" That wasn't a news station. We had basic cable, but it was *very* basic, only about twenty channels total.

"Did you turn it on?"

I was about to open my mouth to reply when the cable box responded. At first there was a sort of scrambled zig-zag image on the screen and then it evened out to reveal a blond woman, naked on her knees, with some guy's cock in her mouth.

"Cazzo!" I swore in Italian, staring dumbfounded at the screen.

"You found it." Carrie laughed, understanding what I meant by my tone even if she didn't know the word. "What does that mean?"

"Fuck," I whispered, watching the blond try to swallow the guy's cock to the hilt and doing a pretty damned good job of it. "It's actually also a term for... well... a guy's cock."

"How apropos!" She laughed again, sounding utterly delighted.

"How...?" I managed to get that strangled word out, leaning closer as the blond slid her tongue down to lick the guy's balls, her hand still gripping his dick.

"Jen from across the street called and told me to change my TV to three-sixteen," Carrie explained. "Her six-year-old apparently found it when he was playing with the remote. She'd already called most of her mommy group on campus and they confirmed it too. We've got free porn!"

"I doubt that was her reaction." I laughed.

"No, she was pretty irate, but I, for one, am thrilled." Carrie giggled. "I just hope it's still on when Doc gets home. I'm tempted to call him and tell him to come now."

"No pun intended." I grinned

"Oh every pun intended," she purred. "Look, he's licking her!"

I hadn't stopped looking. The blond on the screen—who reminded me of Carrie with her doll-like features and bronze skin—had splayed herself on a sofa for the guy, who was now eating her pussy like they gave out medals for enthusiasm.

"She looks like she's enjoying it." Most porn I'd seen was incredibly fake. I hated the girls with the breast implants and fake nails, and the guys were mostly non-entities, just disembodied cocks. This was different. The girl's body was real, full and lush. Her breasts were big, but didn't defy gravity—instead, they kind of spread out a little when she leaned back. The guy was sexy too, his cock big but not enormous. *I could fit that in my mouth.* The thought made my pussy twitch.

"Don't you?" Carrie inquired curiously. "I love having my pussy licked."

I swallowed and admitted it. "Yes."

"Oh my God, Dani..." Her words trailed off as I watched the blond pull her knees back, exposing herself. She wasn't shaved and she was a real blond, the hair between her legs a dark honey color. That reminded me of Carrie too. "This is amateur porn. I wonder...?"

"Wonder what?" Oh God, he was going to fuck her. He positioned himself between her thighs, shoving one leg back so the camera could get a better view while he slid his cock up and down her slit.

"I wonder if this is real. Like real-time, right now. *Live,*" Carrie breathed.

"It can't be," I argued, but imagining that these two were somewhere having sex, right this very moment, was beyond exciting. All the porn I'd seen—Mason had brought some home a few times from the video store—was either vintage stuff with horrible music tracks or the aforementioned fake-sex fake-people type. This felt *real.* Even their sounds were real.

"What if it is?" The excitement in her voice was catching. "Doesn't that turn you on?"

I hesitated, watching the guy on the screen slide his cock into her, and then breathed, "Yeah."

"Oooohhh yeah, like that," Carrie murmured softly into the phone. It was almost as if she'd gotten so lost in the scene she forgot I was there. "Fuck it nice and slow."

I gulped, my pussy throbbing now, insistent. When Mason and I had watched porn, we always ended up in bed halfway through the movie and never finished it. He liked to watch me touch myself first while we watched, and it was almost like my hand had a memory or mind of its own, slipping under the waistband of my shorts.

"Oh I want a cock," Carrie moaned softly. *Me too,* I thought, my fingers slipping through my wetness. "It makes me want to go get my vibrator."

"You have one?"

She laughed. "Don't you?"

"No."

Carrie gasped. "Oh my God, you have to get one! I'd let you borrow mine but I use it too much to let it out of my sight for more than twenty four hours."

That made me laugh, but I also flushed at the thought of Carrie playing with her vibrator. That was far sexier than the movie. "Want to go get it?"

"Really?" She sounded breathless.

"Why not?"

She hesitated and then asked, "Will you play too?"

"I don't have a vibrator," I reminded her, although my fingers were already busy stroking my aching clit. The girl on screen was rubbing hers too.

"You can still touch yourself."

"Okay." I reddened, not telling her I already was. "Can't let good porn go to waste."

"My thoughts exactly! Hang on."

I crooked the phone between my ear and shoulder while she was gone and slid my shorts and panties down. If I was going to play, I wanted full access. I made sure the blinds were closed—I didn't want to give the neighbors a show—and stretched out on the couch.

"I'm back," Carrie said. "I hope it doesn't cut out on us right in the middle or anything."

"That would suck," I agreed, dipping my fingers deep into my pussy and drawing out my wetness.

"So to speak." I could hear her grin. The guy on screen was getting sucked off again. This time they were in a sixty-nine position, her on top. "Oh Doc loves it like that."

Imagining Carrie and Doc in that position made me rub myself a little faster. I heard something over the phone—a soft buzzing noise.

"Is that... your...?" The sound seemed to go right through me, sending shivers straight to my pussy.

"Mmm hmmmm." She moaned softly. "Oh, it's so good."

"I'm jealous," I admitted, watching as the girl on screen turned around on her man and started to ride him. "I wish I had one."

"You could come over," she invited, sounding half-teasing—but half-not.

"Nah, I'll just make do with my fingers," I said, swallowing hard. Why did I turn her down? I wondered, imagining her over there, just on the other side of that wall, fucking herself with her vibrator.

"Fingers are good too." Carrie's breath was coming faster. "Oh yes, nice and hard now... like that..."

"I can't believe we're doing this," I murmured, more to myself than to her, but she answered anyway.

"Me neither, but I can't seem to help it."

I sighed with pleasure, my fingers rubbing fast. "I know what you mean."

"Feels too good to stop," she panted.

"Uh huh." There was no way either of us was going to stop now.

"Oooo look at that!"

I was. The blond had her bottom up in the air, reaching her hands back to spread herself open, and the guy was pressing his cock against the tight crevice of her ass.

"That's just wrong." I winced as the girl squealed, panting, begging him, "Go slow, go slow!"

"Haven't you ever done anal?" Carrie exclaimed. "Oh Dani, you don't know what you're missing."

"You've done that?" I gulped.

"Oh yeah." She moaned softly and I wondered what she was doing. I mean, I knew what she was doing, but I wanted to know *exactly*. Where were her hands? Were her panties on or off? Did she have a shirt on? I wanted to know but was too shy to ask.

"What does it feel like?" I inquired, curious. Mason had never been interested in anal sex so it had never really occurred to me as something to add to my sexual repertoire.

"Well, there's a trick to it," she explained. "You have to use lots of lube. And, like she said, you have to go real slow."

I looked back at the screen, at the size of his cock—and the stretch of her asshole. "I should hope so."

"But only at first. Once he's past that little ring of muscle, it doesn't hurt. And then... oh then..." Carrie moaned again. "I can't even tell you how good it is."

"Really?" I was excited in spite of my misgivings. My clit throbbed under my fingers.

"Try it for yourself," Carrie urged.

"Uhhhh..." I bit my lip.

"Go ahead," she teased. "Just use a finger."

"Ummm..." But I did it. I slowly slid my wet fingers down to tease my asshole. It was small, puckered, very tight, but wet from the juices running down my slit.

"Are you doing it?" She sounded very excited.

"A little," I admitted.

"Get it wet first. That helps," she said. "Just rub it."

"Mmmmm." I closed my eyes, rubbing, just like she said. The skin was very sensitive. It wasn't like touching my clit, or even being fucked. It was very different—but still good.

"See?" Carrie asked. I could hear the smile in her voice. "Now try pressing it in. Just a little bit."

The blond on screen was being pounded in her ass now. I marveled at how it stretched. Was that even possible?

"Ohhh!" I gasped as my finger slid in, up to the knuckle. "It's so tight!"

"I think that's why Doc likes it so much."

I bet, I thought, imagining the two of them doing that. My ass clenched around my finger in response.

"But why do *you* like it?"

Carrie groaned and I knew she was touching herself, using her vibrator. I wondered if she had it in her ass. "Because it makes me come so hard I nearly pass out."

"Wow," I breathed, feeling my pulse between my thighs, fast and hard.

"Look at her face," Carrie insisted. "She really likes it, you can tell."

You could tell. The girl on the screen had her eyes closed, her lips slightly parted, and she was rubbing her pussy while she was being fucked in the ass. So I did both, too, thumb of my one hand in my pussy, finger rubbing my asshole, while I circled my clit with the fingers of my other hand.

"Oh God," I moaned. The sensation was heightened with my finger in my ass and I knew I was close.

"Oh yes," Carrie panted. "Do it, Dani. Fuck your little ass."

"Oh fuck." I closed my eyes, my hips bucking up, picturing her on the couch just on the other side of the wall, touching herself too.

"Yes, fuck yes!" Carrie cried.

The girl on the screen joined our cries of pleasure and I think she was really coming, from the look on her face. The guy pulled out of her ass right then, aiming his spurting cock toward the slight gape of her hole.

"I'm gonna..." Carrie's warning turning into moaning and I was right there with her.

"Yes, yes, yes, me toooo..." I panted, my whole finger buried in my ass, my clit thrumming with ecstasy. I heard Carrie gasping for breath, away from the phone—she'd probably dropped it—and wished I was there to see her orgasm.

"Mmmmm. That was gooooood." She was back, her voice close again.

"Wowwww," I agreed. "You think Jen across the street took advantage of her free porn?"

Carrie snorted. "I think she probably called the cable company to complain about her free porn. Some people don't know a good thing when they've got it."

I sighed. "That's the truth."

"Oh no!" Carrie protested and I opened my eyes to look at the screen. Sure enough, it was back to scrambled zig-zags again.

"There goes our free porn."

"Well it was good while it lasted." She sighed. "Damn, there's my other line."

"Go ahead."

She hesitated. "Are you sure you don't want to come over?"

"I've got some reading to do," I replied. "But call me tomorrow or something, okay?"

I could tell she was disappointed when I hung up the phone, but I didn't trust myself to go over there and hang out. I didn't know what it would turn into, and I should be working on my marriage, I reminded myself. Or, barring that, considering Mason's lack of interest in the topic, I should at least be working on my life, on my future. I didn't have time for play and friends and... well, whatever else the Baumgartners might have in mind.

But even I knew that wasn't quite the truth. What I really believed, deep down, was that I didn't deserve them. I couldn't punish Mason or God or anyone else for Isabella, but I could brutally punish myself and that's just what I'd been doing. What I continued to do. What else was there? It was all I knew.

Chapter Three

Once classes started, things got crazy and I hardly saw anyone. Mason didn't call or come home, but that wasn't much of a change from the norm. Carrie called, though. She encouraged me to come over, to meet after class and go out for coffee. Usually I turned her down. Dante was a lot tougher than I'd thought it was going to be—the Italian wasn't a problem, it was the literary interpretation that was killing me—but that was just an excuse. Carrie was the thing I'd broken out of my shell for, the catalyst that cracked the veneer I'd painted over the surface. Now I was desperately trying to crawl back into that shell and somehow piece it together again.

But it wasn't working. Even if I only saw Carrie once a week or so, I thought about her and Doc way more than that. I spent nights trying to bury myself under pillows and covers so I couldn't hear them having sex. I wasn't avoiding the Baumgartners exactly. I think I was really just trying to avoid myself.

When I passed Carrie on the way back from getting my mail one brisk October afternoon—there was a silver row of boxes at the end of our line of apartments—she stopped me with a hand on my arm, reminding me just exactly why I'd cracked out of my shell in the first place. Just her gentle touch through my coat made me shiver, and not from the autumn wind.

"Wow, nice dress!" She eyed me appreciatively. "Going on a date?"

"Coming back from an interview," I countered with a smile. "The last step in the application process for studying abroad."

"How exciting!" She sounded genuinely enthused, which was really nice to hear. It was certainly a change from Mason's reaction. Even my mother was against my going, but that was just because she wouldn't be able to afford to call me every week in Italy and tell me how I'd ruined my life. "Hey, Doc won't be home until late. Do you want to come over and order pizza? I'm jonesing for some Bella's."

I hesitated. I had a paper to write this weekend on Dante's use of numbers in the Divine Comedy, but it was Friday, after all, and Bella's had the best pizza in town. "I have to change first."

"Okay," Carrie agreed cheerfully, getting her mail and following me back to my apartment.

"I hope you're not allergic," I remarked as Jezebel met us at the door, tail swishing. Carrie had never been in my—*our*—apartment before.

"I love cats." Carrie squatted and held her hand out to Jez by way of introduction. Jezebel, like most cats, took her time getting to know someone. She sniffed and twitched and swished, stalked away and then winding her way back. Carrie just waited patiently through these ministrations until Jez nudged her hand to be petted.

"I'll be right back." I tossed my purse, keys and the mail on the table and went through the kitchen into my bedroom. I was nearly stripped down completely when Carrie came in, Jezebel following, both of them startling me.

"Have to pee!" Carrie waved on her way through to the bathroom. I just stood there, seeing her looking at me in my black bra and panties before she grinned and shut the bathroom door.

I pulled on a pair of jeans and a Counting Crows t-shirt while Jezebel mewed at the door Carrie had disappeared through. Even Jez had a girl-crush on her.

"Traitor," I whispered, sticking out my tongue at the cat and sitting on the bed to wait.

"I love your soap." Carrie came out of the bathroom sniffing her hands. "It's so fruity and nutty. What is it?"

"It's Italian." I smiled. "Imported. It has an olive oil base."

"No wonder your skin is so smooth!"

I flushed, remembering the afternoons we'd spent on the lawn when she'd spread oil over my back. "I can give you some."

The words were out of my mouth before I'd even had time to think. The bar in the soap dish was the last of it—unless I wanted to go into the closet in Isabella's room, which I decidedly did not want to do.

"Really?" The glow in her eyes was so hard to resist. "I'd love it!"

How could I say no to that? I got up, moving mechanically toward the door to the second bedroom, sure the doorknob would be made of fire or ice when I touched it. I hadn't been in Isabella's room in over a year.

"Oh, how sweet." Carrie was behind me, glancing over my shoulder at the nursery, all set up still, ready and waiting. Mason's mother had wanted to take it all down when I was still in the hospital and I'd told him I would kill her if she did. He'd somehow managed to stop her. I think it was the one and only time he'd said 'no' to his parents, aside from making the decision to marry me in the first place. And so it had stayed for the past year and a half.

"It looks like Pepto-Bismol threw up in here." I looked around at all the pink—the walls, the comforter in the crib, the stuffed animals lined up on the windowsill. "Why did I buy so much pink?"

It wasn't just me, though. Once we'd seen the ultrasound and had announced it would be a girl, nothing arrived in any other color.

"What happened?" Carrie asked gently, looking at the picture on the dresser—a tiny baby on a pink blanket, eyes closed, mouth slack, so obviously lifeless.

"Isabella." I breathed her name. How long had it been since I'd spoken it out loud? I turned to open the closet, giving myself something to focus on. "She was stillborn."

"Oh no." Behind me, Carrie gasped. "Dani, she's so beautiful. She looks just like you!"

She did—thick dark hair, the same little rosebud mouth and sooty lashes. She was the prettiest baby I had ever seen. Even the dark hue to her lips, so unnatural in a newborn and caused by the blood pooling, just served to accentuate her beauty, as if someone had rubbed her lips with kisses before sending her to me. I didn't know if her eyes were dark like mine, though. She'd never opened them.

I blinked back my tears, finding the soap in a box up on the shelf and grabbing two bars. "Here. Let's go."

Carrie put the picture back on the dresser and I saw her eyes filled with tears too. "I'm so sorry."

"Me too." I swallowed, holding out the soap, and she took it. "Come on."

She followed me out and I felt a little bit of relief when I could shut the door behind me.

"You don't want to talk about it?" Carrie sat on the bed and looked at me.

"Most people really don't want to hear about it. They say they do, but they don't." I shrugged. "Grief lasts a lot longer than sympathy."

"I know. I've lost three." The tears that had welled up in her eyes spilled over. "But never like that. I can't even imagine."

"I'm sorry." I echoed her own apology to me, sitting on the bed to slide an arm around her shoulder. They were such useless words.

"Just miscarriages." Carrie turned the soap over in her hands. "All before twelve weeks. We keep trying, but..." She shrugged and I saw tears fall onto the soap label, blurring the words.

"A baby is a baby," I said firmly. "Love is love. I loved Isabella just as much at twelve weeks as I did at thirty-eight weeks."

I thought saying her name out loud, making her real like that and bringing her back into this world, would just break my heart into a million pieces all over again. I thought it would take me back to that time when I couldn't do anything but stay in bed and sob, full of leaking milk and love for a baby who would never need it. Instead, I found it almost a relief to be able to tell someone about her, someone who had experienced a pain similar to my own.

"I can't imagine losing a baby at thirty-eight weeks." Carrie's wet eyes met mine. "How do you survive that?"

"I don't know." I shook my head, my hand squeezing her shoulder. "Sometimes I think a miscarriage would be even harder. At least I got to feel her kick and move inside of me. I got see her and touch her. Hold her."

She gave me a sad yet grateful look. "Why do these things happen?"

"Isabella had a knot in her cord." I swallowed, remembering the doctor showing me as if revealing the solution to a mystery—*ah here it is, this is the reason your daughter isn't breathing, kicking, crying, this little knot, like a kink in a garden hose.* Such a small thing, yet enough to kill a child, drive a woman to the brink of insanity, a man to violence. As if anyone could ever solve that mystery.

"Why anyone has to experience that kind of loss?" I shrugged. "I wish I knew."

We were quiet, just sitting there together on the bed, Carrie brushing her tears off bars of soap and me watching Jezebel butting up against our shins for attention.

"Okay, I think we need to take a little trip, you and me." She wiped her face with the end of her t-shirt, standing up and holding out her hand.

I looked at her, bemused. "Where are we going?"

"Margaritaville."

We took a long, extended vacation that night in Margaritaville, and who could blame us? We discovered that we both loved alternative music and turned it up way too loud, dancing around the living room, whirling like Sufis in ecstatic bliss. We had Bella's pizza to fill our bellies, margaritas to numb the pain and music to drown out our sorrows. It was a recipe for either perfection or disaster and I think we delved into a little bit of both.

It was Carrie who took her shirt off first.

"Too fucking hot!" she gasped as she threw it onto the sofa. I followed suit about ten minutes later with my own t-shirt and we danced in our bras, belting out the words to "Teen Spirit" as loud as we could. I don't remember when her pants disappeared. Or mine for that matter. We were doing "Flashdance" imitations in our bras and panties by the time we heard the pounding on the door. "Shit!" Carrie turned the music down, rushing to the door in her underwear. I think the cop who stood outside was more than a little surprised to find two half-naked, sweaty women drinking margaritas and shaking their tail feathers. Thankfully he wasn't really a cop—just campus security—and I think he was fairly distracted by our state of undress, not to mention our teasing. Carrie had clearly talked her way out of a ticket or two in her lifetime and was putting her skills to good use.

"I'm sorry, ma'am, but we had a complaint about the noise." He stood there with his hat in his hands, kind of twisting it around, his gaze skipping from her to me as if trying to find a safe place to look. "Can you keep it down?"

"Oh, we're just having a little fun, officer." She winked and crooked her finger at him. "Want to come in and join us?"

He cleared his throat and blinked really fast. "I'm just trying to do my job, ma'am."

"Ma'am!" She rolled her eyes, glancing over her shoulder at me. "I'm not that old. Do I look like a ma'am to you?"

"M-miss," he stumbled, correcting his mistake. "I just need to ask you to turn the music down a little. I'm sure you can keep on... um... doing what you were doing. Just do it a little quieter."

"Do you want to see what we were doing?" Carrie put her arm around my neck as I came up behind her, pulling me so close I could smell the fruity mix of alcohol on her breath.

"No, ma'am." He shook his head, eyes wide. "Miss. I mean, I just need you to—"

His words stopped when Carrie kissed me. Everything stopped, I think. At first it was just the soft press of her lips, but then her tongue licked at my mouth, seeking entrance, and I couldn't help but give it to her. I moaned softly and wrapped my arms around her, pressed belly to belly. Right there in front of the cop with the door open, standing in bra and panties for the whole world to see, we kissed and kissed and kissed. I felt her melting against me, her breasts molded against mine, and as undressed as we already were, I was wishing for less clothing.

"Want to join us?" Carrie breathlessly asked, turning her face to the cop. I couldn't stop looking at her, the soft curve of her jaw, the delicate stretch of her neck, the way her hair fell over her shoulders. The cop couldn't either. In fact, he looked like he wanted to say yes. He looked like he wanted that very much.

"I'm going to leave now." He took a step back as if to convince himself. "Just keep it down. Please don't make me come back, okay?" He was actually pleading.

Carrie shut the door, giggling, and looked at me. "Well, that was fun while it lasted."

"You're bad." I was still breathless from our kiss, my heart hammering in my chest.

"You have no idea." Her eyes had a very naughty glint and when she reached out and grabbed me, pulling me in again for another kiss, I didn't protest at all. I'm sure it was partially the alcohol, and partially our afternoon of painful confessions, but mostly I think we just both wanted to.

"A threesome would have been fun," Carrie murmured against my neck, her hands trailing down my back. "I have fantasies about cops."

"Oh God, who doesn't?" I groaned when she cupped my ass, sliding a thigh between mine.

"Men in uniform." She sighed joyfully. "Very hot."

I was being pressed back toward the kitchen and pretty much knew where we were going to end up. "But I don't think Doc would have appreciated that."

"True." Carrie reached around and opened the bedroom door. "He's fine with me being with other girls. But other men? Um, not so much."

"So this isn't cheating." I fell back onto the bed with a little exhale when she pushed me.

"Well..." She stretched out beside me in her white bra and panties. We were quite a sight, I'm sure, like an angel in white and a devil in black. Although I wasn't sure which was which at that point. "There's your husband to consider."

"No, there isn't." I slipped an arm around her neck and pressed my mouth to hers to emphasize that statement. She rolled toward me, her thigh sliding up against mine like satin on silk. Her hand moved up my ribs toward my breast and I held my breath, waiting for her touch.

"You're going to tell me what's going on with that some day, right?" she murmured, her lips trailing down my neck, my collarbone.

"Not right now," I whispered, trembling as she feathered kisses over my cleavage.

"No..." She smiled up at me, both hands moving over my ribcage, finding their way to my breasts and cupping them through my bra. "Definitely not right now."

I moaned when she rubbed my nipples through the lacy material. I'd gone to my interview dressed to the nines from my underwear out and I hadn't bothered to change my bra and panties. They happened to be the best set I owned, Victoria's Secret black lace and elegance. Hers were plain in contrast, white cotton bikini panties with a little bow in front and a plain white bra with a tiny pink rosebud in the center, and still I'd never seen anything so sexy in my life.

"I want to make you feel good." Her words had already accomplished the task, but her tongue was trying hard to keep up, lashing at my nipples through my bra, her fingernails tickling my sides. "I want to make you come so hard."

Oh God. My pussy was already soaked from being next to her all night, watching her dancing half-naked, a little drunk, wild and out of control. Those words out of her mouth melted me completely.

"Yes." It was all I could think of to say, but I wanted to give her even more affirmation so I reached around and undid my bra, peeling the straps down my shoulders. Her eyes brightened when my breasts were free and her tongue went back to work, circling my nipples and making me squirm on the bed. I let her do that for while, I don't know how long, experiencing every sensation as if it were the first time. Her mouth was practiced, sure, her hands roaming freely, and just her tongue on my nipples took me to heights I couldn't remember reaching before.

"Here," she whispered, stopping and reaching around, undoing her own bra. "Me too."

It wasn't that I'd forgotten, or that I didn't want to. God knew I wanted to. It was just that she was so beautiful, I wasn't sure I could. It was like touching perfection. I was too afraid I would spoil it. But Carrie wasn't having any of my hesitation or shyness. She guided my hands to cup her bare breasts and the moment I felt the weight of them, the lush curves and the thick arousal of her nipples against my palms, I was lost. Her body became a roadmap I followed behind closed eyes. Touching her brought me almost as much pleasure as her hands on me.

She gave me all those soft, sweet noises I'd heard the night she was making love to Doc, and the sound of them thrilled me beyond words. Everywhere I touched her came alive under my fingers. Her nipples hardened, her breasts swayed, her belly fluttered, her thighs quivered. The exploration went on a long time, and we hadn't even taken off our panties. By the time her mouth made its way down past my navel, the crotch of my underwear was soaked. She nudged at them with her nose, teasing me, making me wiggle. I had no reservations now, no more second thoughts. I wanted her—her mouth, her tongue, her fingers. And she knew it.

She made me wait, teasing my labia with her tongue through the material, rubbing her face against my crotch like a cat. I tried to guide her, my hands finding the tousled mass of her hair and pressing, but she wasn't having any of it. Instead, she nipped at my thighs, making me squeal, and raked her nails gently down my quivering belly.

"Please," I begged finally, not able to stand another minute. "Oh God, please!"

"Please what?" She kissed and licked all around the elastic edge of my panties. "Tell me."

"Please lick me," I pleaded, thumbing my underwear off, feeling it stick at the crotch. She rolled them the rest of the way down and then spread my legs with her palms flat on my thighs, making me moan in anticipation.

"You want this?" She flicked her tongue, barely touching, at the top of my cleft. I shuddered. "Right here?" She used her fingers to spread me slowly open, revealing my clit. I just nodded, gasping as finally, finally, she covered my mound with her mouth, fluttering the soft, hot wetness of her tongue at my center.

"Oh God." It was so good. Too good. I'd waited so long, wanted it so much. Carrie's fingers slipped down to find my entrance, wiggling their way in, first one, then two. My pussy clamped down on her fingers the moment she sucked my clit between her lips. I was going to come. Right now. Right fucking now. "Carrie!"

She drank me in, hungry for more, as I came all over her face. My juices were everywhere, all over her chin, her cheeks, my pussy throbbing with release. But I wasn't done. Nowhere near. When she went to remove her fingers, I thrust against her hand, whimpering. "More. Please. More." She made a delighted noise in her throat, obliging me, giving me her tongue again, concentrating on my still quivering clit. The sensation was almost too much to bear but I pushed past it, through it, riding the wave of my climax toward another.

And then I was there again. It was too much, too soon. I wanted it to last forever, but her tongue and mouth drew another orgasm out of me almost immediately. I bucked and rolled with it, my moans rising to near screams, and she grabbed my hips, trying to keep me steady as I came all over her face. I didn't even know who I was when she kissed her way up my belly to my mouth. I whispered her name, I kissed her back, I remember that, but not much more. I was floating somewhere above it all and it was divine.

It was her body that brought me back to earth again, the weight of her thigh, the shift of her hip. She was all soft curves and gentle valleys, no sharp angles or lines. I began to explore her like she had me, with my mouth, my hands, my tongue. She was so responsive to my touch it was like magic. I traced my fingers down her spine to feel her arch, and rubbed my cheek against her neck to make her tilt her head. She liked my tongue there, over her collar bone, dipping into the hollow of her throat.

I thought she would be in a hurry like I was, desperate to come, but she didn't mind that I took my time, pressing her breasts together in my hands so I could lick her nipples, back and forth, teasing them hard, harder, hardest. She petted me as I stroked her, a hand in my hair, over my shoulder, her fingernails brushing me lightly, making me shiver. By the time I reached the wet stretch of her panties between her thighs, we were both ready for more.

"Here." Carrie moved us and I groaned in anticipation at our new arrangement. She was poised over my face, turned around so she could lick me too. "Better?"

Yes—and no. I wanted to concentrate on giving her pleasure—it had been a long time since I'd been with a woman, although it was a little like riding a bicycle or a horse, I guess. You never really forget how to do it. But every woman was different. I knew I would get distracted by my own pleasure and I wanted to make her feel as good as she had made me feel.

"Oh Dani, you have such a pretty pussy." She kissed and licked at my swollen lips, quickly changing my mind about not liking this new position.

"So do you." I explored her with my eyes first, still shaved smooth. Her labia was thick, just as swollen as mine, her inner lips a hot, deep pink. Her whole pussy glistened with wetness and I fought the urge to immediately bury my face there. "You shaved again. God, it's soooo smooth!"

"Waxed," she replied, rubbing her cheek over my thigh. "Hurt like hell but isn't it worth it?"

"You're braver than I am." I kissed her mound as if to make it all better. "Doc must love it."

"He does," she confirmed. "He says it's the softest thing he's ever had in his mouth."

"Well let's see if he's correct." I pressed my tongue between her pussy lips, tasting her for the first time— tangy and tart, the smell of her like hot musk. I moaned softly at the smooth glide of her labia against my tongue while I explored the soft folds of her flesh. She arched her back, directing me, and I found her clit hiding way up at the top of her crevice. I knew I'd found it when she groaned and rolled her hips, digging her nails into my thighs.

"Your fingers," she whispered. "Put them in me."

I obliged, sliding two of them easily into her slick entrance, feeling her pussy clench. She rocked on my hand, my tongue. There was no stopping her now. She'd been patient until that moment, but when I found her clit with my mouth, she lost it. Something in her snapped and her body went wild, writhing and shivering and rolling on top of me. It was all I could do to hold onto her and keep my mouth anchored over her mound. And she didn't make it easy to focus because with every lick of my tongue, she grew even more eager with her own mouth between my legs. She sucked my clit hard, even raking it with her teeth, making me shudder beneath her.

"Oh fuck!" she cried as I fingered her hard, harder, driving my whole hand against her pussy, giving her as much as I could and she still wanted more. "Oh baby, yes, yes! You're gonna make me come so good!"

She wasn't the only one. My whole body was on fire for her, slick and sweaty and writhing under hers. I couldn't tell anymore what was her fingers, her tongue, it was all sensation, urging me toward yet another climax. I couldn't hold it back and when I felt her thighs quivering against my cheeks, her pussy juices dripping down my chin and pooling at the hollow of my throat, I gave into it, sucking and lapping like a greedy nursling at her cunt as I came, and she came with me too, both of us shuddering with pleasure.

We stayed that way a while, not facing each other, just stroking and petting and purring like two kittens nuzzling each other before a nap. I think it was me who moved first. I got a cramp in my thigh and she massaged it out before turning around and coming up to cuddle. I thought it would be strange, awkward. The alcohol was still in my system, making everything fuzzy, but I knew it was going to wear off and we'd have to think about this in the morning. What we'd done. What exactly had we done?

"I wish you were happy." Carrie traced circles around my navel with her fingernail. "I've never met anyone who deserves to be happy more than you."

I kissed the top of her head. "Except maybe you."

"But I have Doc." Her voice was small, almost apologetic. "And you don't have anyone."

I hated hearing that truth. I almost hated her for saying it. But I didn't, not really.

"I have you."

"Yes you do." She kissed me and sealed the deal.

Chapter Four

I met Carrie at Sweetwater for coffee and a cinnamon roll. It was crowded, as usual, but she had snagged us a table in the back and waved me over when I slipped through the heavy front door, a cold wind following me. There was a nip of winter in it already.

"Cold out there." I shivered, smiling when I saw she'd ordered for both of us already. "Thanks."

"I can't wait for Christmas break." She waved me into a chair, pushing my cinnamon roll toward me. It was thick and fat, the sides dripping with sticky white cream. Perfect. I hadn't allowed myself indulgences like these in the past year, hadn't even considered it. Chocolate, ice cream, pastries, sex—doing anything sweet felt like a betrayal. "Doc has almost a month off. Key West and sunshine, here we come!"

I hesitated, the finger full of frosting halfway to my mouth. "You'll be in Florida for a month?"

"Two weeks," she amended, giving me a little smile and sipping her coffee. "You can come with us if you want."

"No." I shook my head, tearing off a piece of roll. It didn't taste quite as sweet now as I'd hoped. "I've got so much to do over break. My load for my last semester is even heavier than this one, and this one is kicking my ass."

"But then you'll be all done," she reminded me, leaning back in her chair and crossing her legs. She was wearing a skirt, a gray and pink plaid wool one that ended at her knee. Her pantyhose were sheer, her legs long and sexy, still tanned from the summer spent sunbathing.

"Yep," I agreed. *And then what?* I thought. *What happens when I don't have school to do anymore?* When I was pregnant with Isabella, I almost forgot about school altogether. It was Mason who buckled down then. He was an engineering major at the time and had brought home a four-point-oh the semester before she was born. And then we lost her and everything changed. I turned to school, focusing all my attention there, and Mason began drifting, aimless. My red cheeks stung as they warmed, and I swallowed hot gulps of coffee, trying to warm my insides as well, although I wasn't sure that was possible anymore.

"Ugh. Don't look behind you." Carrie wrinkled her nose and bit into her own cinnamon roll.

Of course I looked anyway.

"I said not to look," she warned. But it was too late. There was a woman in the corner with a baby. They'd just come in and the baby's cheeks were red from the cold. *How old?* I wondered. *A year? Year and a half?* Isabella would have been about that age, I guessed. It was like a knife twisted in my belly, every time.

"I don't know which is harder." I turned back to the table. Carrie's gaze was on her coffee. "The little ones remind me of what she was like when she was born, and the older ones remind me of what could have been."

"They all kill me." She poured another sweetener into her coffee and stirred. Sometimes I thought it was like neither of us could get enough sweetness or warmth.

"It sucks." I chewed and swallowed, watching her stir and stir. "Are you guys still trying?"

"Always." She rolled her eyes, licking her spoon and setting it carefully on her napkin. "I set an alarm to take my temperature every day. Poor Doc, I page him when I'm ovulating and he runs home from the hospital hoping he's not called back on an emergency."

I nodded. "But getting pregnant isn't the problem."

"No." She sighed. "It's staying pregnant that seems to be the issue."

"You know, I had some bleeding with Isabella in the beginning," I told her. "The chiropractor gave me this stuff, a sort of cream. Progesterone, I think? I still have some if you want it. Maybe it will help?"

"Sure. Why not? I'll try anything." She gave me a small, rueful smile. "I'd walk on my hands wearing garbage bags and toe socks if it would make a difference."

That made me laugh and her smile widened into a real one.

"Hey, there he is!" Carrie waved at the door and I turned to see Doc coming in, shaking off the cold. My heart leapt and my belly clenched at the sight of him, tall and handsome, snatching off his hat, his ears still red from the cold. "I hope you don't mind, but he got off early and I didn't want to cancel with you."

"No, I don't mind," I replied, which wasn't exactly true, as Doc wound his way through the tables toward us. It wasn't that I didn't want to see him, that I didn't like seeing him. In fact, I think I enjoyed it far too much.

"There's my girl." Doc leaned over to kiss his wife and I looked away.

The mother with the baby had moved and was fully in my line of sight now. The little girl in her arms was dark haired and bundled in a pink coat with fake white fur around the hood. That could have been my life, I realized, watching her wipe the little girl's runny nose with a Kleenex and give her a plastic bag full of Cheerios. Instead I was sitting here with the Baumgartners and Mason was somewhere wasting his life role-playing. I felt a little like I was living an in alternate universe, like Alice down the rabbit hole. Was I living someone else's life?

"Hey Doc." I smiled and greeted him as he waved a waitress over.

Carrie helped him off with his coat. "I didn't order for you because I wasn't sure you were going to make it."

"I wasn't sure either. I had an emergency appendectomy this morning." He looked tired, but his eyes were still darkly bright as he glanced between the two of us. "But here I am."

"I can't wait for vacation." She leaned her head against his shoulder and he slipped an arm around her.

He sighed. "Tell me about it."

They kissed again, more intimately this time, and my stomach did that flip-flop thing. I didn't know if it was jealousy or what, but whenever I saw them like that, my whole body responded like a guitar being tuned, wound slowly to its breaking point.

"You know, I should get going." I started gathering my book bag, shrugging on my coat.

Doc frowned, looking from my half-eaten roll and back to me. "You don't have to leave on my account."

"No, it's not that." I waved his words away, as if he wasn't the reason at all. "I told Mason I would meet him at the apartment."

"You did?" Carrie looked at me in amazement, her jaw dropping.

I shrugged, trying to avoid her gaze. "He wants to talk about our future, whatever that means."

Carrie frowned. "Sounds ominous."

"Or promising," Doc countered, catching my gaze and giving me a little smile.

I shook my head sadly. "Probably the former."

"Dani." He reached for my hand and I let him have it, feeling the warm pressure as he squeezed. "I don't bite."

"I know." I flushed, looking over at Carrie. How was I supposed to handle this, holding her husband's hand in the middle of the coffee shop while she watched? She didn't seem to care and he didn't seem to care. Why was it such a big deal for me?

"I'm sorry I make you uncomfortable," he prompted.

"It's not you, it's..." I pulled my hand away gently, reaching for my bag. "It's the whole situation."

Doc leaned his elbows on the table, his gaze steady, curious. "Is there anything I can do to fix it?"

"I gotta go."

I escaped out into the cold, not looking back. The walk home was long and I trudged the whole way, knowing Mason wouldn't be there for hours. He'd said five but I didn't expect him until six and he didn't actually arrive until seven. I heard the putter of his moped out back while I was finishing up a Lean Cuisine—oriental chicken. I quickly dumped the tray in the garbage and tossed my fork in the sink, nudging Jezebel out of the way to open the back door.

"Hey." He tucked his helmet under his arm, unzipping his jacket. He looked good. He always looked good. It made my chest hurt.

"Hi." I waved him in and shut the door, joining him at the kitchen table. "So, what's up?"

I knew it was something. He never called, and if he showed up, it was always unannounced, sneaking in and out of the apartment like thief. When he left me a stiff message on the machine saying, "We need to talk," I knew I had to be on my guard. And I was.

He put his helmet on the table, leaning back in his chair. "I've been thinking about this Italy thing."

I stiffened, prepared, but for what, I wasn't quite sure. "And?"

"I can't go with you."

I nodded. This was nothing new. "Okay."

"But I don't want you to go." He worked the strap on his helmet nervously. *Snap, unsnap. Snap, unsnap.*

"Now we're right back where we started."

"I know." *Snap, unsnap.* "There has to be a way to fix this."

I shook my head, nudging Jezebel under the table with my foot. She was purring, heading for Mason, getting ready to say hello. "We've been saying that for over a year, long before my going to Italy was even a question."

He lifted his gaze to mine. "We could try therapy again."

"We didn't do anything but fight in therapy." I was just pointing out the obvious. The guy his parents had paid for hadn't done either of us much good. He had an office that smelled like patchouli and sat in a chair that squeaked every time he shifted in it. Mason and I sat on an equally squeaky brown leather couch while the therapist nodded and asked, "How did that make you feel?" every time we said something. It felt useless, like talking to a mirror.

Mason tried a smile. "At least we were talking."

"Yelling," I countered.

He tried again. "Communicating."

I snorted. "I don't know if I'd call that communicating."

"What if we got back with each other? If we moved in together again?"

"Do you want to?" That suggestion took me aback. I sat and contemplated it, having Mason back here. What would that be like? What would we be like together? The memory of him in my bed was too close.

He reached across the table and took my hand. "I want you."

"I want you, too." It was barely a whisper. I looked down at his hand covering mine and knew it was true. I'd always wanted him, even when I convinced myself I didn't, but the gap between us was much wider than the expanse of the kitchen table, and I wasn't sure it was so easily bridged.

"Let me back in." He didn't beg or plead, but I heard the longing in his voice.

"It's your house too. More, really, since your parents pay for it." I brought it up like a shield to put between us. It was a sore point, one of those things we'd always argued about, even before Isabella.

"That's not what I mean." He sighed. "The other day, we were... it was almost like before."

I swallowed, shaking my head. "It will never be like before, ever again."

"I want to fix it." Now he really was pleading. I didn't look up, didn't want to see if the emotion choking his voice was in his eyes. "That's all I want. I want to turn the fucking clock back. I want her back. I want *you* back."

I pulled my hand slowly away, leaving his alone clenched in a fist in the middle of the table. "It's not possible."

"You think I don't know that?" he choked. "You think I don't spend every minute of every day hating myself for not being able to save her? Save you?"

I tried to make myself as small as possible in the chair. "I don't need saving."

"The hell you don't." He slammed his fist on the table, shaking it and making Jezebel startle against my feet.

"I don't know what I need," I told him honestly.

Mason pressed his palms flat against the table. "You don't need to run away, that's for damned sure."

"I'm not running away." I folded my arms and tried not to glare at him.

"Yes you are!" He threw up his hands, rolling his eyes. "You've been running away since it happened!"

"I was mourning!" I snarled, feeling a headache beginning to throb behind my eyes.

"You think I wasn't?" he snapped back. We were both glaring now. "Did it ever occur to you that I might be in pain too? You think I left first? Fuck you! You've been gone since she died!"

I took a deep, shuddering breath, leveling my gaze at him. "Her name is Isabella."

He cringed like I'd hit him. "She was my daughter. I know her name."

"She *is* your daughter," I corrected softly. "So why don't you ever say it?"

"She's gone, Dani." He put up his palms—*I give up.* "I can't bring her back."

"I know that." God knew, that was something that never left my consciousness. "But why do we have to pretend she never existed?"

"I didn't let them take it down, did I?" he hissed, waving toward the bedroom door. "All her things are still in there just like you wanted them—like a... like a shrine!"

I swallowed and blinked at him, trying to keep my voice from shaking and failing miserably. "That's why you left."

"No." He sighed and tried to look away, but our eyes locked together and wouldn't let go. His voice came out as hoarse as mine. "I left because of everything... because it was all broken. You were broken. I was broken. And I couldn't... I just couldn't fix it."

"You still can't," I reminded him in a small voice. "No one can."

We listened to the refrigerator hum and the clock over the kitchen sink tick in the silence between us. Jezebel took the opportunity to jump up onto the table and stalk back and forth between us.

"Maybe we should move back home." His suggestion came out of left field and I knew then that this was it. This was the thing he'd really come to talk about, to tell me.

"What?" And still it shocked me. The idea of going back to our tiny hometown four hours away from here, the place where we'd both attended high school, where we'd made out in the cramped backseat of his little Escort, where our parents continued to live their very different, very separate lives, was so anathema to me, it actually made me nauseous.

"My dad's offered me a job."

I stared at him, agape. I couldn't say anything.

"Fixing up houses and flipping them." I think he mistook my silence for agreement. He just kept talking. "There's good money in it. We could get our own place. Start again. Try again."

Try again. Oh my God, he meant try to have another baby. A replacement baby. Now I really was nauseous.

I took a deep breath, getting the words out as calmly as I could manage. "I'm going to Italy, Mason."

"You don't have to!" He raised his voice almost to a yell and I gave it right back to him.

"I want to!"

His jaw clenched, unclenched. "So you want to leave me?"

"You left me first," I snapped.

"I beg to differ on that point."

I shoved Jezebel off the table as she tried to settle on the table between us and she mewed at me in protest from the floor. "Mason, I'm not going to live off your parents anymore. I don't want that kind of life."

"You don't have a problem with them paying your rent now!" he growled.

I gaped at him and then stood, the chair falling over behind me to the floor, making Jezebel bolt for the bedroom. "If you believe that, you don't know anything about me!"

"I know everything about you!" He grabbed my arm as I started after the cat, jolting me around so I was facing him. "I know that you can't stand being wrong or hurt. I know you wish you had died instead of her."

"Stop it." I tried to shake him off me, but he held my arm in a bruising grip.

"I know that you love me!" he yelled, shaking my arm, making my teeth rattle.

I glared up at him, using my other hand to push against his chest. "Love doesn't solve anything! I loved her and *she died*. I loved you and *you left*. What the fuck does love do for me? *Nothing!*"

Mason grabbed my other arm, the one shoving him, and held me still. "Come home with me."

"To do what?" I was shaking all over. "So you can work for your parents, so we can live their lives? That's like asking me to live in quicksand! I want my own life! Don't you, Mason? Don't you?"

The look in his eyes almost melted me. Almost. "I've never wanted anything but you."

"I can't do this anymore." Even as I said it, I realized it was true. Enough. I'd had enough. "You're never going to grow up are you, Peter Pan? Do you want to live in Neverland forever? Are you going to spend the rest of your life playing games and pretending bad things don't happen?"

"I'm trying!" he croaked.

"Trying isn't good enough." It was a painful truth and he didn't want to hear me, pretended I hadn't spoken.

"I'm trying to make a life for us—for you!" He shook me, hard, and I struggled to get away. "A job, a house, a baby—isn't that what you want?"

"No!" I yelled, giving it back to him. "I want *us*. I always wanted us. I don't care what you do, as long as it's yours. Don't you understand that?"

"Nothing is ever good enough for you!" He let me go, walking away, pacing. "Jesus, my mother was right!"

"Your mother?" I gulped, trying to breathe.

"She warned me you were a gold digger. That you got pregnant on purpose. She warned me not to marry you."

I knew she'd never liked me, but this! His words made me go cold inside.

"And I did it anyway." He paced, talking to himself. "Because I loved you. Because I thought you loved me. Because the baby..." His voice broke and he ran a shaking hand through his hair. "You know they think it's your fault? My mother swears it was all that freaky yoga stuff you were doing, that you killed her!"

He lifted his twisted face to me and I saw his tears. "Not that it matters. They don't believe she was mine anyway."

I went after him, screaming like an animal. I don't remember anything I said, although I know I said things, and he did too. He shoved me away from him into the wall, knocking the wind out of me and I sat there, dazed, the world going in and out of focus, not sure if the pounding I heard was on the door or in my head.

"Dani!" Someone was calling my name. "Open up! Dani! Are you okay?"

It was Doc pounding on my front door. I struggled to stand and Mason stepped aside as I moved to open it.

"Sounded like you might need a little help over here." Doc's jaw worked as he looked past me toward Mason. Doc was wearing just a sweatshirt, no jacket, his breath making white mist in the cold. He must have heard us yelling and run over in a hurry.

"Mason was just leaving." I swung the front door wide, letting Doc in.

"Is that so?" Doc's big bulk filled the doorway, his gaze fixed steadily on my husband.

Mason looked just at me, his voice soft. "If I walk out that door, it will be for the last time."

I didn't say anything. Instead I walked to the back door, opened it and waved him through. When I shut it behind him, I turned to find Doc behind me, his face filled with concern.

"Are you okay?" He looked like he wanted to say something else, maybe reach for me, but was holding himself back.

"No," I whispered, telling him the truth. Then I collapsed in his arms and sobbed.

He carried me to the couch. At least I'm pretty sure that's how we got there, me in his lap, my hot face pressed against his neck. He rocked me and patted me and shushed me for a long, long time. I couldn't stop crying. I hadn't cried like that since Isabella was born, when my eyes had been so swollen I could barely open them and I had to ice both my face and my breasts to keep the swelling down.

"What happened?" Doc finally asked when my breath had settled into occasional hitches.

"It's over." I sniffed, wiping at my face with the sleeve of my turtleneck. It was no use—I'd soaked them both. "Not that it wasn't already. I don't know. I just wish it all could have been different."

"I'm sorry." He rocked me some more and I felt him kiss my hair. "You've had it rough, Dani."

"I guess so." I was feeling even more sorry for myself, hearing the sympathy in his voice. I lifted my head to glance at the clock. "Carrie must be going crazy."

"She's at her pottery class," he assured me. "If she'd heard what I did before I came over here, she would have been knocking on your door with a baseball bat."

I laughed. "She's heard us before."

"But she wasn't sleeping with you then."

I blushed. "About that..." They were both so matter-of-fact, but it made me want to crawl under the couch or something.

"I just thought we should talk about the elephant." Doc smiled, his eyes bright.

"The... elephant?" I blinked.

"Yeah, you know, the pink one in the middle of the room?"

I tried not to laugh. "Oh, that one."

"I just want you to know it's okay." He tucked a strand of tear-wet hair behind my ear.

"She said you were okay with it," I admitted in a small voice, still not quite believing him.

"I am." He nodded, turning my chin so he could meet my wandering eyes. "I really am."

It was hard to believe, but she said it and he said it, and what other choice did I have? "Okay. I believe you."

"Good." He looked satisfied. "Now, when you move in with us..."

I startled. "What?"

"Trust me on this." He grinned and I nearly melted into his lap. His smile was infectious. "You're going to come home with me now. When Carrie gets back, I'm going to suggest you stay, and she's going to agree."

"No, wait, I..." I protested, even tried to get out of his lap, but he held me firm, his arms wrapped tightly around my hips.

"Yes," he insisted.

"But Doc..." I shook my head.

"No buts." He put a finger to my lips, silencing me. "I just want you to know that you're more than welcome. No strings attached. You make Carrie happy, and that makes me happy. Okay?"

What else was there? "Okay."

"Good." He slapped my hip playfully, giving me a nudge. "Now let's go."

I stood, looking down at him, perplexed. "Where are we going?"

"If I let you stay here, Carrie will string me up by my giblets, and I'd rather keep those intact, thank you very much." He winked and stood, waving me onward. "Now get your coat."

Doc had been right on. Carrie was furious with Mason and clucked over me, and when Doc suggested I stay, she picked up on the idea like it had been her own, insisting. Doc grinned, shrugging when I looked at him, like he was saying, "I told you so." I slept on their sofa that night.

I could hear them through the wall. *What did they make these apartments out of anyway,* I thought, *balsa wood?* I hugged a pillow over my head and buried myself under the comforter Carrie had covered me with, trying to block out the sound, but it was no use.

I rolled onto my back and looked up at the ceiling in the dark. There was a full moon and the blinds were open a little, making shadow slats. I turned over and tried again to sleep. It wasn't an easy task, considering I couldn't stop thinking about the time I'd spent in the very bed Doc and Carrie were now having sex in.

I thought it wouldn't matter, knowing she was married and with him. At first, I thought it would probably be just one night anyway, two drunk college girls doing a little experimenting. Neither of those things turned out to be true. It did matter, and it wasn't just one night. I couldn't stop seeing her, wanting to be with her, touch her. Doc assured me he was okay with all of it, but how could that be true? And what did he think of me?

I sighed and sat up, hearing the sound of Carrie having her second orgasm of the night. It was her fourth in two days, at least as far as I knew. I'd made her come twice yesterday—once in the shower on my knees and another time in the bedroom, sitting on my face. The memory of her over me, spreading her pussy with her fingers, made me feel weak, like I couldn't possibly stand up. But I did anyway, making my way over to their bedroom door in the moonlight. It was closed and I hesitated, hearing the rhythmic sound of the headboard. They weren't done.

"Oh fuck, baby, you feel so good!" Doc's voice. I flushed at his words, closing my eyes, picturing them. Was she on top? Was he? Maybe he was behind her, doggie style. She liked that. She told me so. "Easy clit access," she explained. She liked being licked that way too, hips up, breasts pressed into the mattress.

"Harder!" she gasped. "Give me that cock!"

I wanted to see and my hand clutched the doorknob but I didn't turn it. I could hear them, the hot pant of their breath, the slick slap of their bodies together.

"Don't you wish it was Dani's pussy, baby?" Carrie purred and I heard him groan. "Do you want to fuck her while she licks me?"

"Oh, hell yes," he growled. The pounding of the headboard sped up. He was really fucking her now. I blinked at their words. Carrie had hinted at a threesome and had told me they'd done it before, but I had no idea that she and Doc had actually discussed having one with me.

"She's got such a sweet pussy for you." Carrie went on with the fantasy. "And her ass... oh God, it's so tight. She's never had a cock in her ass."

He gave a strangled, animalistic cry. "Would you let me fuck her ass?"

"Yes," she promised. "And I think she'd let you too. I think she wants it."

I swallowed, pressing my ear against the door, wondering if what she said was true. Would I let him? Being with Carrie didn't feel like cheating on Mason— although how I could imagine he'd been faithful to me and our marriage for the past year and a half was beyond me. I didn't really believe it, but for some reason, I'd felt obligated to stay faithful, even if he wasn't here, even if he hated me. For a long time, it had been easy, but Carrie had changed all that. Now I wasn't only unfaithful, I was falling for her. And jealous of her husband. What was wrong with me?

And Mason's gone...

He had been gone, but now he was really gone in a way he hadn't ever been before. It was out in the open, a stated thing. The pink elephant had been unveiled.

"Oh wait, wait," Doc moaned, but I could tell he was going to come. All guys got that sound in their throat, deep and guttural, at the point of no return.

"Come in her hot little ass," Carrie said hoarsely. "Do it! Now!"

It sounded to me like he did as she asked because the headboard hit the wall hard, once, and he grunted several times, low and loud, the sound of his climax resonating somewhere deep in my lower belly.

"Oh God." Doc panted. "That's too fucking hot. Do you really think she's going to?"

"I think she will," Carrie mused. "Right now it's just us girls, but I think she'll come around. Besides, who wouldn't want you?"

He chuckled. "You have a point."

I heard someone get up and then the sound of water running. I thought about it, still breathless from listening to them having sex. What would it be like, to be with both of them? It had been so long since I had been with a man other than Mason. Would I be able to put him out of my head, to keep myself from comparing them? Being with Carrie was different. There was no comparison and it was all about the pleasure.

I pressed my hand against the wall as if I could touch them. There was something about Carrie. Maybe I'd unconsciously known that she had experienced a pain similar to mine. Or maybe it was my own sexual reawakening that had catapulted me into this position and she was just a catalyst. Being with Carrie had stirred something in me, but I instinctively knew that being with the Baumgartners, Doc and Carrie both together, would color in a world I'd been living in black and white.

I didn't know if I could go back to living in a world filled with color, a place of infinite beauty but ferocious pain. Was it really worth the risk?

Chapter Five

"I was too superstitious to buy anything the first time." Carrie opened the bedroom door—the second one, the one you had to walk through their bedroom to reach. "And after that, well, I guess I didn't see the point."

The room was empty, just as she'd said it was—no crib or wall hangings. It wasn't painted pink or blue, and it was musty from being closed up and unused for so long. There weren't even curtains on the windows.

"I'll have to get Doc to put up some blinds." She frowned at the uncovered window.

"I have some." They were still in my closet, waiting for Mason to take down our white sheet-curtain. "I never put them up at our place. Are you sure about this?"

Carrie took my hand and squeezed. "I don't want you to go back there."

"He won't come back." I was pretty sure of this.

"I think he will." She pressed her lips together and crossed her arms. "And I don't think you should be there when he does."

"Maybe you're right." There was no point arguing with her. "And Doc's okay with Jezebel?"

"He's more of a dog kind of guy, but he loves animals," she assured me. "He's fine with it."

I touched the door frame, frowning. "But this room should be for..."

"It's yours." She snatched at my hand and squeezed it again. "I want you here. Please stay."

So I did. We left the bed at my apartment. I wasn't even thinking of it as *ours* anymore. Instead, the Baumgartners bought a futon. I brought a small dresser and a little writing desk. Carrie laughed at Doc, calling him He-Man when he tried to carry it all by himself, negotiating the corners first through my place and then theirs. When it was done, we ordered a pizza, drank beer and watched a Red Wings game. I nestled between them like it had always been that way while Jezebel sat in the window and cleaned herself, looking up occasionally when we interrupted her by cheering at the television.

The strangest thing was bed time. I had to pass through their room to my own, and seeing them snuggle together was the hardest part of my night. Well, almost. They tried to be quiet, I could tell, but Carrie didn't have a "mute" button when it came to sex, and eventually, I think they forgot themselves, forgot about me. That was the hardest part.

Other than that, living with the Baumgartners was easy. Jezebel adopted Doc like he was her long-lost familiar, or maybe the other way around, waiting for him at the window and twining herself around his feet, trying to trip him the moment he came in the door. I don't know what Carrie did while I was in class, but she was always happy to see me when I got home, no matter what mood I was in. She was like that with Doc, too, and she was an amazing cook. No more Lean Cuisines for me.

The best thing was playing. That's what Carrie called it, "playing." Not just sex, which there was plenty of between the two of us—Doc was gone so much it gave us ample opportunity—but really playing. Like two little kids, we'd run around the apartment in our underwear tagging each other with squirt guns Carrie brought home on a whim from the dollar store.

We got into tickle fights—my feet and the backs of her knees. And the first time it snowed, we made angels.

"I wish there were real angels." Carrie reached over to me with a mittened hand and squeezed my gloved fingers as we rested, splayed in the snow, mouths open to catch the big, fat flakes that fell all around our faces. It wasn't even Halloween yet, so it was a wet, heavy snow that would probably disappear tomorrow or the day after when the fickle weather decided to warm again.

"That's what my mother told me." I snorted. "Don't worry, Dani. Isabella's with the angels now."

She sighed. "That would be comforting, wouldn't it?"

"I wish it was."

Carrie sat up and exclaimed, "Let's make a snowman!"

And that's what we did. It was huge, as tall as we were, and we draped it with a purple scarf and gave him a drooping carrot for a nose and stony black eyes. His hands were branches we shoved mittens on and his mouth was made out of strands of red licorice. When Doc got home, Carrie told him she was sorry, but there was another man in our lives now. She giggled as we gathered at the back door to look out at our new guy in the fading sunlight and Doc praised our mad snowman-making skills.

"If you have to throw me over for someone, it might as well be the Brad Pitt of snowmen. Look at that six pack!"

"It's more like a keg." Carrie laughed, sliding her hand under his sweatshirt and I got a glimpse of Doc's belly, which was nicely toned.

Doc grinned. "Hey, if a six-pack is good, a keg is better, right?"

We ate chili that night and I tried to study on the couch while Carrie and Doc snuggled at the other end of it under a blanket and watched MacGyver.

"Oh, I got our costumes," Carrie said during a commercial.

"Uh-oh." He looked sideways at her. "Please tell me I'm not going as Dr. Frankenstein."

"Nope." She grinned. "You're going as Dr. Hawkeye Pierce and I am going as Hot Lips Houlihan."

He laughed. "Well I guess that's better than Dr. Dolittle."

"Hey, I could have gone with Dr. Frank-N-Furter." She stuck out her tongue and I tried to imagine Doc dressed as a transvestite. "Or Dr. Spock."

"I'd wear fishnets for you." He nuzzled her neck. "Or big ears."

"You could go as Dr. Scholl," I chimed in and they both laughed. "You have to go as doctors?"

"It's the Halloween costume party at the hospital," Doc explained. "Everyone has to go as a doctor or a patient."

"Dani, you still have to get your costume." Carrie nudged me with her foot.

I shook my head, burying myself back in my book. "Not me."

"Are you gonna make me pick it?" She nudged me again, making a face.

"Are you really gonna make me go to a costume party?" I groaned. "I won't know anyone there."

"Neither will I." She petted my thigh with her instep. "We can get drunk and embarrass Doc in front of all the other residents. Doesn't that sound like fun?"

"Come on, Dani." Doc winked at me. "Come with us."

Damn that man had a sexy smile. "Maybe."

"I'm picking your costume." Carrie brightened. "How about a sexy nurse? Or, let's see... Dr. Who? Dr. Strangelove? Dr. Kevorkian?"

"I liked the sexy nurse idea," Doc chimed in and gave me another grin when I looked at him. Every time he looked my way, it made me feel hot.

"Go ahead," I mumbled. "Pick whatever you want."

"Does that mean you'll come?" Carrie urged.

I shrugged. "Maybe."

"Tease." She poked me with her pink-painted toenail. "Come with us. Besides, you don't want to be stuck here passing out candy to toddlers in cute costumes all night, do you?"

"I'm gonna head to bed." I closed my book and stood to stretch.

"I'm sorry," Carrie apologized and I gave her a brief smile.

"Nothing to apologize for," I replied. "I'm just tired." Which was mostly true. Besides, I liked to get into my room before they did so I didn't have to walk through theirs while they were in bed.

"Goodnight, Dani," Doc called as I went past.

I let out my pent-up breath when I got to my room. It felt as if my whole body was buzzing. I didn't know how much longer I could live here with them, like this. The tension was palpable, and not in a bad way. I kept trying to hide it, but I was attracted to Doc and I think he knew it. I think they both did.

Maybe if I dressed up and pretended to be someone else, I thought sleepily as I crawled into bed with a book I didn't really intend to read, I might have the nerve to actually do something about it.

Of course, I never intended to go half-naked, but that's just what happened. I didn't go as a doctor, or even a sexy nurse. Carrie decided I should go as their patient, so I got to wear a hospital johnnie and fuzzy bunny slippers. She let me have a creamy silk robe with a tie to cover that, but she didn't let me wear any panties. Or a bra.

"It has to be authentic," Carrie teased as we got ready in the bathroom that night. She was in green army fatigues with "Houlihan" written on her pocket. She made a sexier "Hot Lips" than Loretta Swit ever even thought about being. "Besides, I can do this..." She slipped a hand into one of the openings in the back, squeezing my ass.

I squealed. "Yeah, well so could anyone else!"

"It's no shorter than some skirts I've seen you wear."

Well, that was true. Thankfully the weather had changed for the warmer and the snow had completely melted. Carrie was so excited about the "authenticity" of my costume that it was hard to disappoint her by putting on panties. I was already buzzed, which helped, although Carrie made the suggestion completely sober. She had refused and was apparently immune to Doc's magical pre-party margarita mixing, which helped convince me it really wasn't *that* much different than wearing a short skirt out. And I'd done that before without panties.

Doc drove and I sat in the back, worrying the whole way that I wasn't going to know anyone. But it would be a good excuse to sit in the corner all night, I reasoned. There was no way I was going to get up and dance in this getup. Carrie kept teasing me that I could meet some cute, eligible doctor—and it occurred to me that perhaps her costume choice hadn't been just a last-minute idea.

"I'll let you off at the door." Doc pulled up and whistled when I got out of the car and the wind blew my robe open, making me shiver. "That's quite a view, Ms. Stuart!"

I flushed, pushing Carrie ahead of me. "I swear, I'm going to kill you."

"I wish everyone I treated looked as good in that outfit!" he called before Carrie shut the door.

"I'll stay behind you until we get in." She giggled and let me go forward.

The party was at a hall and it was in full-swing by the time we got there. There were latex gloves all over, blown up as balloons. They even stuffed them with ice and put them in buckets to keep the wine cold.

"What's your poison?" the bartender asked as I backed my way carefully onto a stool, making sure my "flaps" in the back were closed. I looked up at the bar and saw a painted sign, "Name Your Poison," on the wall.

"Fuzzy navel," I replied, watching Carrie greet Doc at the door. He made a dashing, rakish Hawkeye and he slipped an arm around her as they made their way toward me.

I laughed when the bartender poured liquor out of test tubes. They'd really gone all-out. Doc ordered a drink but left it at the bar when Carrie grabbed his arm, saying, "I love this song!" over the din and dragging him onto the dance floor.

"Nice costume." A guy wearing scrubs sat next to me as the bartender served me up another fuzzy navel. I figured I needed the liquid courage. He was kind of cute in a nerdy doctor sort of way. "I love the slippers."

I smiled down at the bunnies. "Thanks. Harvey and Bugs. They're out on a day pass."

"So you're dressed up as a mental patient then?" He admired the rabbits when I waggled them, but I think he was really more interested in looking at my legs. When I raised an eyebrow at him, he replied, "Because with that body, there can't possibly be anything physically wrong with you."

I laughed. "How many women wearing hospital gowns have you tried that line out on tonight?"

I was actually not the only one wearing a hospital gown, I'd noticed, which was both a relief and kind of a letdown. It was always fun to be original, but on the other hand, it was less embarrassing when it was the standard uniform. Of course, I wondered how many of those were going around Commando.

"I'm Ben. Want to dance?" he offered. I hesitated, glancing out at Doc and Carrie. She had her arms around his neck and they were slow-dancing now. Seeing them together made my chest hurt.

"I'm Danielle." I introduced myself and then said, "Okay," when he held out a hand. I let him lead me, but when we got out there, I was careful not to put my arms too far around his neck. I was all too aware of how high the hospital gown rode up when I did that. The dance floor was dark except for the disco-ball overhead and the song was something slow and Top-Forty that I didn't recognize.

I was already buzzed and I let him slide his hands down past my waist, putting my head on his shoulder and breathing in the scent of him—alcohol and cologne. It had been a very long time since I'd been in another man's arms besides Mason's. It made me heady.

"What are you wearing under this?" he whispered into my ear.

"Nothing." I smiled, my eyes still closed.

I heard his breath catch. "That's what I thought."

"Can I cut in?" I looked up to see Doc tapping Ben's shoulder. Ben didn't look too happy about it but he yielded, stepping out of the way and accepting Carrie's arms around his neck.

"I see you met Ben." Doc slipped his arms around my waist. I felt him pulling the flaps closed tighter. "Not that I'm surprised. He's quite the ladies' man."

"I'm sure he thinks he's charming," I murmured, resting my head against his chest. Doc's scent was very different, earthy. Much more masculine.

"I have no doubt," he agreed, glancing over at his wife who was laughing at something Ben had said. "So why were you dancing with him."

"Jealous?" I blinked, looking up at him with a half-smile.

His eyes darkened and his nostrils flared "I guess I'm protective of what's mine."

"*She's* yours," I reminded him. "I don't belong to anyone."

"Yes you do." His arms tightened and I actually gasped for breath. The way he looked at me made my insides go all soft.

"Are you staking a claim?" I inquired, still breathless.

His lips moved against my ear. "Do you want me to?"

"Right here? Right now?" I teased. His hands were still moving, lower now, caressing the rounded curve of my behind.

"Anywhere." His breath was hot as he crushed me to him, letting me feel how hard he was. It made my knees weak. "Any time."

I pulled away, dizzy. "I just felt like dancing."

His hand moved up against my lower back, his smile slow. "Next time, come get me. I'll dance with you."

"Okay," I agreed. We traded off all night—me, Carrie and Doc—dancing in every combination possible. I forgot about my costume and its limitations, although I'm sure I flashed more than one person that night. Ben took the hint and let the three of us do our thing, watching from afar. I saw him leave with a redhead who filled out her sexy nurse uniform quite nicely, but I was pressed against Carrie on the dance floor at the time and didn't look back.

"Let's go home," Doc murmured on the other side of his wife as he watched us rubbing against each other. He'd apparently done enough elbow-rubbing and chatting about golf—he didn't play, he said, but he knew the lingo—and I saw the look in his eyes. I'd glimpsed it often enough before he took Carrie into their bedroom.

"Up front." Carrie directed me when we piled in the car. Doc was driving, Carrie in the middle. The Cadillac—another one of Doc's "indulgences"—had a bench seat and we all fit without a problem. Doc put the heat on. I was shivering, although I wasn't entirely sure it was from the cold.

When Carrie slid her hand under my gown I didn't protest. I did glance over at Doc to see if he was watching, though, and he was. Instead of shying away, I spread my thighs wider for her probing fingers, moaning softly when she found my clit.

"Good girl," Carrie whispered, leaning over to kiss my throat, her lips warm and soft. She strummed me with her thumb and slipped her fingers down my wet slit, seeking entrance.

"Oh God." I whispered the words into her hair as she began to finger me, glancing over at Doc, flushed with embarrassment. Thank goodness it was dark outside. It was bad enough, being half naked in front of him and his friends all night, but watching him look at me with his wife's eager fingers fucking my wet cunt was too much. "Please, Carrie, wait..."

"Nuh-uh!" She was up on her knees, undoing her pants and sliding them down. I stared as she got them off, her panties, too, grabbing my hand and pressing it between her thighs. She was soaked—almost as wet as I was—but I tried not to give in.

"When we get home," I pleaded, looking over at Doc again. I saw him shift in his seat, eyeing us but not saying anything. Then his gaze shifted back to the road.

"Please," she begged, rocking against the hand cupping her mound. "I can't wait. I can't. I have to come."

I groaned, giving in and working my fingers against her clit. She sighed in happiness, her hand doing me too, the sloppy wet noise of our pussies being fingered filling the car. I could smell her, and me too. We were sweaty from dancing and wet with our own juices, pungent and strong.

"Oh yes, yes." Carrie rolled her hips, giving me more access, and I took it, thumbing her clit while I fucked her with my fingers. She straddled my thigh, steadying herself against the back of the seat, her fingers never stopping on me. I bit my lip, feeling my pussy starting to clench. "Oh Dani, yeah, your pussy is so fucking hot!"

"Oh no, no, please, you're gonna make me come," I begged, wanting it, not wanting it. She fucked me furiously, her body working against mine, and I cried out in pleasure, my head rolling back on the seat, feeling my cunt clamp down around her pumping fingers again and again.

Doc groaned and shifted in his seat again. But Carrie wasn't done. She lifted her wet fingers to her mouth and licked them, and then she leaned over and put them in Doc's mouth. He made a low, growling noise at the back of his throat, eagerly sucking the taste of my pussy off her hand.

I turned my face away, but Carrie undid the buttons of her shirt and pulled down her bra, letting her breasts free. They spilled out against my cheeks and she rubbed them against my face, making me squirm and grab at them to keep from drowning. My hands were covered with her juices.

"Suck them," she begged, holding them for me now, pressing her dark, fat nipples as close together as she could. "Please. Please!"

I took one of her nipples into my mouth and then used my tongue to lash at the other one, back and forth between them, eager and hungry. She began to touch herself, rubbing against my bare thigh, and then she reached around to undo the tie of the hospital gown I was wearing, yanking it down over my shoulders to expose me. Doc glanced over again, and this time, in spite of Carrie doing her best to obstruct my view, albeit totally unintentionally I was sure, by writhing in my lap, I saw his hand rubbing and cupping the crotch of his pants.

"Does it make you hot?" Carrie whispered, splaying her pussy against my leg, her fingers buried deep. "He's hard for you."

I whimpered in response as she pushed me on my back onto the seat, my head resting near Doc's thigh. I looked up and met his eyes and saw the way his gaze traveled down my body in the darkness, the streetlights flashing like lightning, giving him a view of my nearly nude state. The hospital gown was just around my waist now and Carrie spread herself over me, sucking hard at my nipples, her pussy rubbing wetly over my leg.

"Jesus," Doc whispered, watching his wife situate herself above me, half-sitting, scissoring our legs together on the seat. She shoved one of my knees back to spread me open wide and I held it for her, the slick velvet press of her pussy against mine too delicious to resist.

"Like that?" she murmured, looking down into my eyes.

"Oh God yeah," I agreed, rocking my hips with hers. This was something we'd never done before and although the position was awkward and the movement of the car didn't make it easy, I wasn't about to tell her no, not now. I didn't care if Doc was watching. I didn't care who was watching. I didn't even care if we got pulled over and thrown in jail, as long as I got to come with her cunt spasming against mine.

I looked up to see Doc's hand fondling his wife's breast, pinching her nipple. The sight made me crazy with lust and I rolled my hips, rubbing our swollen pussy lips together. Carrie glanced down at me, her eyes half-closed in pleasure, and then she looked back at her husband.

When she licked her lips and focused on his crotch, I knew I was in trouble. "Take it out, Doc."

He didn't argue. The sound of his zipper seemed incredibly loud. Then there was a low, rhythmic shuffling sound. He was touching himself. I wanted to look, but I didn't. Instead I closed my eyes and concentrated on the sensation between my legs. Carrie knew just what she was doing, teasing my pussy lips open with hers, making our clits kiss softly in the dark.

"Oh baby," Carrie murmured, rocking faster, harder. "Oh fuck, I'm gonna come all over!"

I looked up at her riding me, her lower lip pulled between her teeth, Doc's hand on her breast. I prayed the other one was on the steering wheel and not on his cock, but I didn't look. Instead, I covered his hand with mine, rubbing her nipple as she started to come. I heard him gasp before she started to keen and wail with her orgasm and then he groaned again when I guided his hand down to cup my breast instead.

"Please," I begged, looking up at him, meeting his dark eyes for a moment before he glanced back at the road. "I'm so close. Play with my nipples."

His hand was huge, his palms hot, cupping and kneading my breasts. Carrie was still coming, not letting up, shoving me into the seat with her thrusts. When Doc squeezed my nipple between his thumb and forefinger, I could somehow feel it right against my clit. I moaned and arched, calling out his name and then hers.

"I'm gonna come!" I cried and let myself go between them, my pussy clenching like a vise with my climax. Carrie collapsed, kissing me and laughing softly. Her lips were warm and I could still taste me on her mouth where she'd rubbed my juices over her lips.

"Doc's turn," she whispered, moving up and reaching for his cock. I turned on the seat so we were belly to belly, her ass against the back of the seat, mine turned toward the dashboard. She slid herself closer to him and I watched, my breath caught, as she began to stroke him.

His cock was gorgeous. It literally made my mouth water and I whimpered softly when I watched her lick the head. He had one hand in her hair, the other on the steering wheel. Carrie glanced at me and saw the look in my eyes.

"You want some?" she offered, tilting his cock in my direction. I swallowed hard, looking at the way it curved in her hand. Did I want some? I glanced at Doc, who could barely keep his eyes on the road, his gaze skipping over my nude body pressed belly to belly with his wife's, stretched out on the front seat of his Cadillac. He had a look in his eyes like he was dreaming. I imagine I did too.

"Mmmm." Carrie took him back into her mouth with a hungry, sucking sound. I heard Doc's sharp intake of breath and saw his hand tighten in her hair, pressing her down on his dick. She worked him with her fist and mouth, making lusty noises and twisting against me on the seat. It was driving me crazy. Maybe she knew that because she looked over at me a few times, tilting his cock again, an offer.

Christ. Pretty soon I wasn't going to be able to resist. I think she knew that, too. Instead of giving in to my lust for Doc, I slid down onto the floor on the passenger's side and nuzzled my way between Carrie's thighs. She lifted her leg for me as I suckled her pussy, lapping at the swollen lips that had been pressed against mine just moments before.

"Carrie, God, that's so fucking good!" Doc moaned, his eyes half-closed. She squeezed his dick, making him jump.

"Don't get us into an accident," she warned, the mushroom head of his cock spilling over with glistening pre-cum. I could see it in the flash of a streetlight and then it was dark again.

"I promise," he panted. "Just please don't stop."

"I won't," she whispered, going back to work. I did too, sucking slowly at her clit and watching them together. The danger of what we were doing, Carrie and I completely exposed as we sped along the highway, just added to the excitement. She squirmed on the seat and I pressed my palm flat against her lower belly, feeling her muscles twitching.

"Oh fuuuuuck!" Doc groaned and I felt the car slowing, taking a corner. He glanced down to see my mouth attached to his wife's pussy. "That's good, Dani. She loves being licked. Suck on that little clit."

I made a little noise in my throat in agreement and so did Carrie. She tasted so good in my mouth, and I knew I was swallowing our juices all mixed together. Her clit throbbed against my tongue and I spread her with my fingers so I could really get in there. It liked to hide when she was really excited and I didn't let her escape, twisting and turning with her as she thrashed on the seat.

"Oh fuck! Oh fuck!" Doc slowed the car to jerky halt and Carrie really started pumping him hard and fast into her mouth. I couldn't help it—I slipped my hand down and rubbed myself off while I watched, sucking on Carrie's clit, the same hot, wet rhythm she was keeping up on his dick. A few fast, furious circles around my swollen clit was all it was going to take.

"Carrie," he warned, panting and thrusting up into her throat. She gagged on his length but didn't stop. In fact, she went faster still, swallowing so much of him that she buried her face against his crotch. "Oh God! Now!"

Now. Now. My pussy spasmed under my flying fingers as I drank Carrie's pussy in. She bucked against my tongue, coming too, Doc's cum spilling out around her lips and flooding down the length of his cock. She didn't let much escape, still shuddering from her orgasm, finding it all with her tongue and licking it up.

"Taste," she whispered huskily, pressing her fingers to my lips. My mouth was still fastened to her pussy, but I obediently opened up and took her fingers in, looking into Doc's dark eyes as I tasted his cum. His gaze filled with lust as he watched me suck her fingers.

"We're home," he managed, still breathless.

"I'll say." Carrie nuzzled his thigh, her hand moving in my hair.

As soon as we started straightening and tucking, putting clothes back in place, somehow the spell was broken. I rushed into the house before them, heading straight to my room, and pretended to be asleep when Carrie knocked and opened the door to check on me.

I wanted to say something, but I couldn't. Instead I actually tried to sleep, rolling around on the futon that seemed too hot and small that night. When I heard her cries and the rhythmic sound of the headboard slapping against the wall, I wanted to go to the door and open it, to slip into their bed and join them.

What in the hell are you thinking? I chastised myself for my lust, for wanting him, wanting her. I wanted both of them. I stretched and rolled and sighed, longing to be in bed with the Baumgartners as they sucked and fucked each other in the room next to mine.

I rolled and stared up in the darkness. There was a vent, high up near the ceiling. These were old apartments and I didn't know what kind of heat they had, but the vents were big and wide. I could see light spilling into my room from theirs. No wonder we could hear everything. There was nothing between the walls at all.

I heard every word, every sigh, every moan and thrust. I knew that if I did what I really wanted, if I crept into their bed, they would both welcome me. If I hadn't known it before that night, I knew it for sure then. But for some reason, I couldn't. I'd always done what I wanted, had gone against what everyone said I should do, but I couldn't admit to anyone, even myself, that I wanted this.

Instead of taking my pleasure, I stole it, sliding my hand down under the covers to touch my aching clit in the dark. I closed my eyes and imagined me with them, between them, Doc's hands, Carrie's mouth, both of them on me, in me, taking it all. I rubbed myself frantically, throwing my arm over my mouth and moaning into my own elbow to keep them from hearing, knowing they could probably hear me anyway as I thrashed on the bed, my knee hitting the wall as I spread myself wide and thrust up against my hand.

I came when I heard the short, sharp sounds of Carrie's orgasm and nearly passed out when she cried out my name—and then he did too, as if they were calling me to them through the darkness. Still, I denied myself and didn't go, burying myself under the covers and trying to drown myself in sleep until morning.

Chapter Six

I agreed to meet Mason at Sweetwater. That was my compromise—the Baumgartners insisted that I not see him alone, that it be in a public place. I wouldn't let them come in, so they sat in the car parked at the curb, feeding the meter while Mason and I talked.

"Dani, I'm sorry." Mason didn't drink coffee so he ordered a Coke, drinking it from the glass. "The things I said..."

I waved his apology away, shaking my head. "Forget it."

"I'm going to move home after this semester." He stated this flatly, not looking at me. I'd known, when he asked me to go with him, that he was going to. He did whatever his parents wanted him to do, and this was clearly something they wanted. "I told you, my dad offered me a job. And I'm not really doing much here."

He looked at me sheepishly and I didn't deny it. He'd been failing more classes than he passed since Isabella was born. His parents didn't do anything about it except around report card time. Then they lectured and threatened for a phone call or two—but they still paid the rent and the groceries and put spending money in Mason's account every month.

"Okay." I glanced out the window and saw Carrie looking in. I knew she was worried. "That's fine."

"The apartment..." He swallowed. "My parents won't pay for it anymore after Christmas break. We'll have to move our stuff out."

I felt my breath go away. It wasn't the thought of moving out—I'd basically done that already. I could find my own place and get a job to pay for it. That wasn't the problem. It was Isabella's room—her things. What was I going to do with those?

I swallowed and lied. "Okay. That's fine, too. I'm already practically moved out anyway."

He stared at me. "What?"

"I'm living with the Baumgartners." I saw the shock and anger on his face and was glad, then, that Carrie had insisted on a public meeting. "They think it's not safe for me, living at the apartment alone."

"Fuck you, Dani." Mason's jaw worked, his eyes flashing. "You know I wouldn't hurt you on purpose."

I pushed my full coffee cup away. "Let's not do this."

"I just wanted to tell you in person." He leaned back in his chair and I didn't want to look at him. He was too sad. "I thought we could at least do this thing without fighting."

"Lots of people have amicable divorces." I shrugged. "It's the 'in' thing."

He paled. "No one said anything about a divorce."

"What do you think we're doing here? Playing house?" I scoffed.

"Dani, I..." His face fell. I didn't want to see this, do this. I desperately wished I was somewhere else. "I love you. That has to count for something."

I swallowed and looked out the window. Carrie saw me and waved, but I didn't wave back. When I looked back at Mason, he had tears in his eyes. I thought maybe I could muster a few, just for show, but I think I was all cried out. I'd emptied myself completely after losing Isabella. I just didn't have anything left.

"I love you too." I said the words. I even meant them. "But we don't work together. Maybe we never did. Maybe your mother was right—we only got married because I was pregnant, and now that there's not a baby anymore, well, what's the point?"

"We're the point." He leaned forward, giving in one last college try. "We could have a life together."

I shook my head. "We want very different things. Don't you see that?"

"What if I came to Italy?"

"Then we'd be unhappy together in Italy." I smiled at him sadly. "And you don't want to move any further away from your family. You want to move closer, not further."

He sighed. "Then let's just leave things open."

"We can't live like that."

"We have been," he argued.

"And it's been the year from hell," I reminded him. "At least for me."

"Me, too."

I wanted to touch his hand, to hug him, but I knew it wasn't the best thing for either of us. "We both need a direction."

"Can't we go in the same direction?"

"Not anymore." I grabbed my purse off the back of the chair, slinging it over my shoulder and standing. "I've got to go."

"So I guess we'll move everything out...?"

"Tell your parents I'll get my stuff out over break." The thought made me go cold. "They won't have to pay for me anymore."

"I wish..." He stood, putting his arms around me, and I let him, trying not to cry. He didn't have to say it.

"Me too."

"How did it go?" Carrie turned to me as I got into the backseat—after the other night, it was much safer back there. She looked sympathetic, but she kept casting suspicious glances at Mason. He was still sitting at the table, drinking his Coke.

Doc glanced at me in the rearview mirror. "You don't look so hot."

"I have to move out of my apartment."

"Well, we can get the rest of your things." Carrie sounded relieved. I think the thing she'd been most afraid of was that I'd get back together with him, and that obviously hadn't happened. "That's not a big deal. He-Man over here can handle it all himself, I'm sure." She smirked.

"By the power of Grayskull!" Doc cried, pulling out and merging into traffic. He had a rare Saturday off. Carrie laughed and punched him lightly in the upper arm.

"Yeah, but I have to..." I swallowed, looking out the window at the cars passing by. "Isabella's things. They're all still..."

"Oh, sweetie," Carrie sighed, peering over the seat at me. I didn't meet her gaze. Maybe if I didn't think about it, it would all go away. That tactic hadn't gotten me much of anywhere over the last year and a half, but as a momentary coping skill, it worked just fine.

"We'll work it out," Doc said firmly and I tried to smile at his attempt to fix things when he looked at me again in the rearview mirror. "Don't worry."

Right. Like it was that simple.

"Maybe we shouldn't have our surprise today," Carrie murmured, talking to Doc.

He glanced at me again, and then at her. "Maybe."

"What surprise?" I perked up, leaning over the seat.

She hesitated and then half-turned toward me. "I planned a little surprise for your birthday."

My birthday wasn't until next week—November sixteenth. "What did you plan?"

"I know it's not until next week, but this is Doc's only day off until Thanksgiving, so..."

She knew I couldn't resist. "What is it?"

"It wouldn't be a surprise if I told you." She grinned back at me and then turned to Doc. "What do you think? Yes or no?"

"I don't know." Doc hesitated.

"Don't I get a vote?" I looked between them. "I vote yes!"

Carrie laughed. "Are you sure?"

"Yes!" I insisted. "A surprise will be good for me."

"I guess we'll see."

I couldn't imagine what the surprise could possibly be. They'd already been more than generous with me, and I hoped it wasn't anything extravagant or crazy that I'd have to turn down. Carrie knew how I felt about accepting things from Mason's parents, even though I did it anyway out of necessity, so I figured she'd know I wouldn't accept any expensive gifts.

I didn't have to worry.

"Where are we?" I stared up at the building as we passed, remembering a billboard I'd seen on the highway for this place—the one with the half-naked girl wearing leopard print.

"The Landing Strip." Carrie giggled at my expression. "Haven't you ever been to a strip club?"

"No." I stared at her, then at Doc. He was parking the car. "This is my surprise?"

"I hope you like it." She took my hand as we got out.

"Have you been here before?"

"We've come here a few times." Now I knew why Carrie had taken such an interest in my attire before we left, insisting I wear a skirt. She wore one too, almost as short as mine. It only came to mid-thigh. "They have a whole couples section."

"They do?" And here I thought the only people who frequented strip clubs were businessmen, college guys and drug dealers. It was mid-afternoon, but inside it turned to night. The bar was dark, the lights over it dim. It wasn't anything like I thought it would be. The guys weren't leering or cheering. There were a few men in suits and ties seated around the stage, almost casually, but as I observed them watching the show, I noticed they looked at the dancer like a lion looks at a gazelle—just before it pounces.

The brightest point in the room was on the stage, wrapped around and sliding down a silver pole. She was topless, wearing the tiniest black g-string I'd ever seen, but aside from that, she wasn't what I would have imagined in a stripper. Her breasts were small, not tiny but definitely not fake, with tiny pink areola and nearly flat nipples. I couldn't help wondering what they looked like when they were hard and suddenly wished it was colder in here. She was petite and pretty, certainly. Blond, so maybe that fit the stereotype, but her hair was long and straight, more Marsha Brady than Traci Lords. Her legs looked deceptively long in her heels and she had a tattoo on her hip, some Chinese lettering.

Carrie had a better body—hell, so did I—but it wasn't about that. It was the way she moved, like a cat, a snake, curling around the pole, writhing. I'd never seen anyone move their hips like that, even in porn.

Doc paid the cover charge. The music was loud, pounding, and it vibrated my pelvis, which was probably the point. I looked around at the clientele and saw that I hadn't been far off in my stereotyped assumption. There were mostly men seated at big, padded black leather benches around the stage, sipping on drinks and occasionally glancing up at the dancing girl. Personally, I didn't know how they could keep their eyes off her, but maybe that was just because it was all new to me.

"Over here." Carrie led me by the hand and I stumbled after her. We took a booth in the corner. There wasn't a bad seat in the house if the girl on stage was the main attraction—and she obviously was. Doc slid in, sandwiching me between them, and waved a waitress over to order drinks.

That's when I noticed that the waitresses were topless too. Ours was pretty, her curly brown hair pulled up away from her face, revealing stunning dark eyes, but I doubted her customers looked at her face very much. Her breasts were far too distracting.

"What can I get you?" She didn't have a pad or a pen—where would she put it? *Must have a great memory*, I thought, as Doc ordered two shots, Carrie ordered a Cherry Coke, and I asked for a seven and seven. I couldn't help watching her walk away to get our drinks. Her g-string was practically invisible.

"What do you think?" Carrie whispered.

"It's... interesting." I couldn't take my eyes of the girl up there. Everything about her screamed sex, from the way she whipped herself around the pole to the long stretch of her legs when she bent over, dragging her hair across the stage. It was like watching porn in public and I squeezed my legs together against the gentle pulse of my pussy between my thighs.

"Sexy, isn't she?" Carrie handed my drink over when the waitress brought it.

I sipped and nodded, welcoming the warm burn of the alcohol down my throat and the dizzying buzz it sent to my head.

"Anyone hungry?" Doc asked as the waitress slipped away. My gaze followed the sway of her hips as she walked by. I glanced around, amazed to see businessmen eating sandwiches and hot wings with their beer. How could anyone watch a show like this and even think about eating?

"Not for food," I managed, gulping down the rest of my drink.

"I know what you mean." Carrie smiled knowingly, sliding her hand over my knee under the table. I shivered but slid closer to her so our thighs were touching.

"Here." Doc reached into his back pocket and pulled out his wallet. I stared as he opened it to reveal a wad of dollar bills. He grinned at me. "I came prepared." He handed a few over to me and nodded toward the dancer. "Go put one in her g-string. Everyone should do it at least once."

I blushed. "I can't."

"I'll go with you." Carrie nudged me, snatching another dollar from Doc's hand. "Come on."

We slid out of the booth and moved toward the stage. The girl had seen Carrie flash her dollar out of the corner of her eye and started toward us, using her hips to propel herself forward, her pelvis jutting out, her belly undulating as she walked. It was an amazing performance and I stood, transfixed, looking up at her as she neared us.

I could smell her—something light and fruity, sweet. Carrie winked at the blond as she tucked the dollar bill under the elastic strap of the dancer's g-string and I noticed for the first time that she had several more under there. I couldn't move, entranced by her hips, the slightly rounded expanse of her belly and the piercing—something I'd never seen before at all—in her navel.

"Hi, sexy." She squatted down in front of me, her eyes warm and dark, like chocolate. "Welcome to the Landing Strip."

She obviously knew I'd never been there before. "Th—thanks," I managed to strangle the word out of my throat and she smiled, a slow, seductive thing, as she gracefully got to her feet, her black heels impossibly tall, making her legs look as if they never ended as she stood over me. She was so close I could see the fine little blonde hairs on her thighs that she'd missed while shaving. That sight made my knees weak.

"Got something for me?" Her hips swayed, the triangle of material between her legs cupping the swell of her mound as she moved back and forth. She was completely nude except for that one swath of material and I couldn't think about anything but what was beneath it.

She turned around and got down onto her knees, flipping her hair over her shoulder to look back at me. Stunning. Like a little goddess. Her thighs were parted and she rocked as if fucking an invisible cock coming up through the stage. She moaned softly, really giving us a show, and I stood enthralled, my breath just gone.

Then she moved toward us, crawling backwards, until her bottom was right in my face. She rolled her hips, showing us far more than she was probably supposed to—I saw a glimpse of her pussy lips, her pink slit, and the wink of her asshole—before cocking her hip toward me for her reward.

I would have put a thousand dollar bill in her g-string if that's what had been in my hand. Her skin was velvety smooth as I tucked the bill under the elastic and I ran a fingernail over her skin, following that g-string line, and saw her smile as she stood, dancing her way back toward the pole in the middle of the stage.

"How do you like your surprise?" Doc asked, grinning as I floated back to our table.

"I love it," I exclaimed as I picked up my drink and swallowed the heat—Doc had ordered more for me while Carrie and I were otherwise occupied.

"Well, this isn't all of it, actually." Carrie smiled slyly. "You still get your birthday lap dance."

I gaped at her. "My what?"

I'd heard of lap dances, of course, but thought they were sorts of things that just happened for bachelor parties. Of course, before the Baumgartners, I didn't know couples went to strip clubs, either. I was wrong on both counts. Doc and I had quite a few more drinks and the dancers changed shifts—the new girl had blond hair with dark roots and obviously fake breasts and didn't interest me nearly as much as the other dancer had.

And Carrie knew it. "Let's see if we can get you a lap dance with Tiffany."

"Tiffany?" I blinked.

"The girl who was up there before this one," Doc explained.

Tiffany. If that wasn't a stripper name, I didn't know what was. Lucky for us, Tiffany was still around and said she'd be happy to do a lap dance for us. Doc paid the lap dance fee—neither of them would tell me how much it was—and the bouncer let us into the private back room.

My knees were trembling as we went in. I was glad there was a half-moon booth seat we could sit on together while we waited.

"How does this work?" I whispered. I was surprised the bouncer hadn't given us any instructions.

"Technically, we're not supposed to touch her," Doc explained as I looked around the dark little room. There was a black curtain drawn on both sides, but the music was piped in through speakers on the walls. The lighting was dim, but we could all see each other clearly enough. "Although sometimes they let you. Just don't touch her unless she invites you to."

"Dancers tend to be a little more free with us girls." Carrie winked. "Oh, and they can touch you. And they will. A lot."

I flushed. "Can we touch each other?"

"Technically, there's no rule against that." Doc grinned.

Tiffany came into the room like she owned it—and I guess she did. She was wearing more clothes than she'd been in before, a short-short silvery dress that glittered when she walked. Her heels were silver too, and even higher than the ones she'd worn on stage, if that was even possible. She wasn't a tall girl, but those shoes made her legs look delightfully long and curvy.

She moved slowly, deliberately, hips swinging. Her gaze met mine as she edged closer. I could smell her again, that heady scent, as she leaned toward me, putting her hands on my bare knees, which were primly squeezed together under my short skirt. She had tiny hands, with long delicate fingers and lightly painted nails.

"I hear you're the birthday girl." She nuzzled my neck, nosing my hair out of the way so her whispered words could brush my ear. "I'm Tiffany."

I cleared my throat, feeling her nails lightly tickling my knees. "I'm Danielle and this is my friend, Carrie." It felt very strange to be introducing myself to a stripper, but I looked over and saw Carrie smiling. "And her husband, Doc." On the other side of me, Doc was quiet, not smiling, just watching, his eyes dark.

Tiffany rocked as she started to stand, her little hips moving back and forth, her hands trailing up the silk of her thighs, lifting her dress, just a little. She teased us, her hemline flirting with her g-string as she danced, using her hands to trace the soft curves of her body through the material. I heard my own intake of breath when she cupped her own breasts, rubbing her palms flat against them until her nipples grew hard.

"Isn't she pretty?" Carrie whispered. I felt her hand cupping the back of my neck, massaging. "Does she turn you on?"

My mouth was too dry to speak as Tiffany began to grind her hips in circles, slowly spiraling downward toward the floor and then back up again, giving us more glimpses of her panties. Next to me, I heard Doc give a little groan as Tiffany stayed down on the floor, thighs open, palms pressed to the floor, doing that same motion I'd seen her do on-stage, as if she was riding a nice big cock. I was pretty sure Doc was wishing it was his.

Tiffany gave a little moan, her eyes half-closed, and then she turned her back to us, up on her knees, reaching back to lift her skirt over her behind with her hands. Her palms slipped the material up and down against her ass, playing peek-a-boo with that tattoo on her hip, and then bending forward onto her hands and knees so we could see her bottom up in the air.

"Mmm." Carrie's hand moved down my back, over to my hip, and I felt her breasts pressing into my side. "That's sexy."

Tiffany rolled gracefully on the carpet, turning and coming toward us on hands and knees, stalking, like a cat. She stopped in front of me—my thighs were still squeezed tight, my pussy pounding between my legs, begging for attention I knew it probably wouldn't get for hours—and then rubbed her cheek against my knees.

She was so soft, so inviting, I couldn't help opening a little. Encouraged, she sidled up between my thighs, making me part them wide, wider. My skirt rode up too high, all the way to my hips, as she situated herself between my legs, rubbing her body against mine.

"Take my dress off," she whispered, her breath hot against my ear.

I groped for the hem of her dress, my fingers brushing her behind through the material. I inched it up and finally reached the edge, finding it almost impossible to concentrate as she continued to writhe between my thighs. When I started lifting, Tiffany gracefully raised her arms and let me slip the silky material over her head.

"That's better." She slid her body against mine from bottom to top, her naked breasts grazing my cheeks as she stood and placed a knee against one of my hips, and then swung her other knee over, straddling my lap. Which was, I reasoned, why they called it a lap dance. She rocked her hips against mine, her hands moving through my hair, down my shoulders, and I wished I was wearing far less, so I could feel the heat of her pussy against mine.

Her breasts were in my face, rounded and sweet, her nipples pursed and hard. It was the hardest thing to not slide my hands over her body, to grab her hips and press her against me. Carrie seemed to know this and she held one of my hands, squeezing gently, as Tiffany ground our crotches together. My breath was coming in short pants and hers was too. I wondered if this really turned her on, or if she did it so often, all day long, that it just became part of the job.

"Here." Tiffany took my hand, the one Carrie wasn't holding, and slid it up her waist, over her ribs, stopping just short of her perfect little breasts. I kept my hand where she left it as she rocked in my lap, watching every delicious undulation of her curvy little body. She made me dizzy with lust.

I wanted to suck her nipple into my mouth as it grazed my cheek, but I didn't. I wanted to kiss her throat as she arched, but I didn't. I wanted to cup the hot little mound of her pussy and rub her, but I didn't. What I did do was slowly move my hand back down her waist, letting it rest where the elastic band of her g-string stretched over her flawless hip.

"Pretty tattoo," I murmured, using my fingernail to trace the lines of the Chinese characters. "What does it mean?"

She slowed, looking bemused as she stared down at me. "*Love is pain.*"

I nodded, rubbing my thumb there. "Ain't that the truth."

"Yeah." Tiffany suddenly felt real in my arms as she leaned in and kissed me. It was a soft, sweet kiss, and I opened my mouth under the gentle press of her tongue. I heard Doc moan softly, watching us kiss, and felt Carrie's hand in my hair, stroking me.

"Don't tell," Tiffany whispered so softly in my ear I thought I might be dreaming, but then she was kneeling between my thighs, spreading them open with her palms and pressing her face against my pussy.

"Oh God." I moaned softly as she started using her tongue through my panties. They were already soaked—I was so turned on I could barely think. Carrie grabbed one of my knees, pulling it back and spreading me even wider, her breath hot against my ear as she watched the little stripper working her face between my legs. Doc followed her example and grabbed my other knee, and they both held me like that, open wide for her hungry mouth.

"Oh fuck," I moaned, my head going back, my eyes closing. Her tongue lapped again and again at the crotch of my panties, teasing my clit, and I knew I couldn't possibly stop the orgasm that was already shaking my thighs. "Oh you're gonna make me come!"

I heard little Tiffany make a noise, her nails digging into my thighs, and that sent me over the edge. I shuddered and climaxed under the onslaught of her tongue, letting Carrie and Doc support me completely in my delirious pleasure. She came up smiling, her eyes bright.

"Don't tell," she said again, glancing at the dark curtain.

"No," I gasped, shaking my head. "I won't."

"I think I owe you..." Doc started to reach for his wallet but Tiffany stopped him.

"It wasn't about that." She frowned at him but then smiled up at me. "Happy birthday, Danielle."

I sat up, closing my legs, my ears still ringing. "Thank you, Tiffany."

"Lynn." She stood, her fingers rubbing at her tattoo. I don't even think she knew she was doing it. "My name is Lynn."

And then she was gone, grabbing her dress off the floor and heading through the black curtain toward the back of the club.

"Oh my God." Carrie slid her arms around my neck, nuzzling my cheek. "Wow."

"Does that happen every time?" I gasped.

Doc laughed. "Hardly."

"Happy birthday." Carrie kissed me softly, reminding me just exactly what I was doing here, between them. I felt Doc's hand moving over my thigh, his arm slipping around my waist.

"Okay, you can take me home and give me my real present now." I looked back and forth between them.

"Your real present?" Doc raised an eyebrow and then groaned when I slipped my hand down to his crotch and squeezed. His eyes brightened. "Are you sure?"

I felt the hard throb of his cock and rubbed him through the material. "How fast can you drive?"

"Faster than you can say 'yes.'"

"Y—" He cut the word off with a hard, probing kiss, and then we were out of there, just as fast as he had promised. I don't remember the ride home. I vaguely remember riding between them, Carrie's hand up my skirt, mine in Doc's lap, distracting him. But he managed to make it without killing us, pulling up to the apartment and quickly killing the engine.

"No running away." Carrie grabbed my hand as we got out of the car and I smiled, but there was no escaping anyway. They had me between them before we even got to the bedroom, Carrie kissing me up against the front closet door, sliding her thigh between mine, Doc behind, his hands moving over both of us at once.

"Oh God!" I cried when Carrie dropped to her knees and shoved my skirt up over my hips, burying her face between my legs. First she licked me like Tiffany had, right through my panties, and the sensation coupled with the memory was almost enough to make me come right then.

"Lick it," Doc instructed her, reaching down to lift one of my legs, holding me open for her and pulling my panties aside. "Bury your face in her, baby."

Carrie moaned and did just as he asked, her eyes wide and wanting as she looked up at us both. I could feel the steel press of Doc's hard cock against my ass and I rocked back against him and onto Carrie's eager tongue, both together, back and forth, the pleasure increasing with every motion.

"Oh please!" I arched, feeling my knees beginning to go, but it didn't matter because Doc held me up, his fingers spreading my pussy wide for his wife's lashing tongue. "Make me come! Oh! Ohhhh!"

Carrie covered my pussy with her mouth and sucked. That did it, the instant change in sensation from licking to suction, and I buried my hands in her hair, rubbing my pussy all over her face and tongue as I came. Doc held me up as I quivered in his arms, too breathless to speak.

"Time for a bed," he insisted, reaching around and lifting me off the ground entirely, carrying me to the bedroom while Carrie followed behind.

He sat me on the bed and I leaned back on my elbows. We stayed that way for a minute, the Baumgartners looking down at me and me looking up at them, their hands in my hair, running over my shoulders, my breasts. I'd lost my heels somewhere, probably during our interlude in the living room, and I put my bare feet up on the bed and let my legs fall open.

"What am I going to do with you two?" Doc groaned at the sight, my panties still pulled aside, my pussy wet from Carrie's attention.

His wife leaned over to kiss him. I saw their tongues and the way she squeezed his crotch before whispering, "Everything," into his ear.

I tugged at Carrie's skirt—*off*—and she obliged, letting Doc unzip it before she slid it down her hips. She was undressed completely when she crawled into bed and she started to take my clothes off too as Doc watched. He peeled off his shirt and I admired the sight of him as Carrie unhooked my bra and tossed it on the floor with the rest of our clothes. All that was left was my panties.

"I want your tongue," Carrie murmured, hooking her thumbs in the elastic of my underwear and sliding them down my thighs. "I want to come in your mouth."

"Sit on my face." I reached for her and she came to me, leaving the last vestige of our clothes on the floor as she straddled my head. The smell of her was incredible and I wrapped my arms around her hips, pulling her down so she was spread wide, her pussy mashed against my tongue.

"You like watching, Doc?" Carrie asked, looking over her shoulder at him. I couldn't see much out of the corner of my eye, but he was still standing next to the bed, his pants and boxers down, his cock fisted in his hand.

"You're so fucking beautiful," he breathed. I felt a hand on my thigh and knew it was his.

"Her tongue feels so good." Carrie faced the headboard, gripping it as she rocked against my mouth. I drank her in as deeply as I could, lapping up her juices, all the way down her slit and back up to the top of her cleft. "Oh God, Doc, her sweet little mouth..."

"Her pussy's sweet too," Doc countered and I moaned when I felt his fingers slipping through the wetness between my thighs. "So smooth. Oh Dani, God, I want to fuck you."

"Do it!" I took my mouth off Carrie's mound just long enough to gasp the words. "Fuck me!"

Doc groaned and climbed up onto the bed, parting my thighs with his big hands. I let him push my knees way back, drowning in Carrie's wetness all over my face. I could tell she was about to come by the sounds she made, the way her legs started to shake.

"Oh wait!" Carrie cried, slipping a hand behind my head and shoving my face against her cunt. Her clit was hiding again and I sucked at it, feeling her shudder and buck. "Oh fuck! Coming! Oh God!" I squeezed her hips, keeping her pressed hard against my face, my tongue working against her quivering clit until she starting begging me to stop.

"Wait! Wait!" she panted, sliding back, away from my eager mouth.

"More." I searched her wetness with my fingers, feeling her tremble.

"Jesus," Doc whispered. I felt his hands on my thighs, gripping so tightly I thought he might be giving me bruises. Not that I cared. "I'm not going to last long."

"I want to watch you fuck her." Carrie turned around, still breathless, stretching out next to me and resting her cheek on my belly.

"You do it." Doc knelt up between my legs and the sight of him made my pussy throb. "Put me inside her."

Carrie grabbed his cock, pumping him slowly in her fist, making his eyes half-close, before she rubbed the head of him right against my clit.

"Oh!" My hips bucked up involuntarily at the sensation as she teased me with his cock head, up and down my slit.

"Are you ready?" she murmured. I didn't know if she was talking to him or to me, but it didn't matter, we were both more than ready. I felt her sliding the fat mushroom tip of him down toward my hole and tilted my hips up to meet him.

"Oh Dani!" He called my name as he shifted forward, sliding his length into me. He stopped there, not quite bottoming out, his eyes closed, his breath fast. "Oh. Wow. Okay... wait."

I felt an incredible sense of power, seeing his face, knowing how turned on he was, how close he must be to just shooting his load right then. So I squeezed my muscles, clamping my pussy down around his shaft, making his eyes fly wide and his cock jerk inside me.

"Brat!" he gasped, using the flat of his hand to smack my hip. I just giggled, doing it again. "Oh fuck. Dani, really. Don't."

"Does it feel good?" I whispered huskily, squeezing rhythmically, first slow, then faster. "Does it make you want to come?"

He gave a low growl and grabbed my legs, pushing my knees back as far as he could, practically bending me in half. His gaze fell between my thighs where his cock was pressed deep into me. Carrie was smiling, leaning on her elbow next to us on the bed, just watching.

"I want you to lick her," Doc told his wife. "Lick that pussy while I fuck her."

Carrie perked up, getting to her hands and knees and leaning over me. "My pleasure."

"Oh! Doc!" I gasped when he slid his cock nearly all the way out and then shoved it back in, deep and hard. Carrie spread me open with her fingers, leaning in to suckle my clit, pulling it into her mouth with a gentle suction and cradling it with her tongue. "Oh my God!"

"Feel good?" Doc gave me a wicked smile, pushing my legs back when they slipped a little, tilting my hips and giving both of them better access to my pussy.

"Yessss," I hissed, biting my lip as he began to fuck me. It was so good I could barely stand it, the sensation of being pounded like that while Carrie's tongue worked fast and furious against my clit. I found her pussy with my fingers, needing to feel her wetness. She opened for me easily, letting me finger her, keeping up the same rhythm as Doc.

"Don't come inside her," Carrie murmured, taking a momentary break from my throbbing clit, making me whimper at the loss of sensation. "I want to lick your cum off her wet little cunt."

Doc groaned and shoved deep into me, bottoming out now, again, again. He was fucking me so hard it almost hurt and I didn't care—I wanted more, my fingers buried deep in Carrie's pussy, my thumb strumming lightly at her little clit.

"You ready for it?" he growled, reaching a hand down between us, close. So close. My pussy was on fire, my whole body tense and begging for release.

"Do it!" Carrie stopped licking me to pump his cock, spreading my pussy lips wide with her fingers and aiming him at my clit. "Come all over her cunt!"

He gave a low keening wail, throwing his head back as he came, and I saw the muscles in his belly clenching, releasing, again and again, a hot gush of cum flooding my pussy. Carrie kept him tight in her fist, squeezing the head and rubbing him against me as she milked him, his cock erupting in her hand.

"Oh that's a lot," she whispered, and then her mouth covered my wet mound, sucking and licking and making me come. I gave into it completely, forgetting about the hand I had buried in her pussy, but she didn't stop, rocking into my fingers, fucking them and bringing herself off too as we climaxed together.

"Too fast," Doc complained with a groan as he collapsed on the bed, looking over at us, still twined together in the afterglow of our orgasms.

"We've got all night," Carrie reminded him with a laugh, climbing over to snuggle on his other side.

"We've got forever," I countered, smiling at them both as I pressed Doc between us and twined my fingers with Carrie's on his chest.

And that night at least, we made good use of our time together.

Chapter Seven

"I got you an early Christmas gift." Doc put the envelope on the four TV trays pushed together in the middle of the living room that we'd set as a makeshift table with plates and silverware and wine glasses.

"Me?" I glanced toward the kitchen where Carrie was putting the final touches on Thanksgiving dinner. "Doc, no."

"Yes." He pushed it toward me, topping off my wine and heading back toward the kitchen. "It's non-refundable so there's no way out. Mwuhahaha!" He grinned as he grabbed Carrie's ass on the way by, making her squeal and poke at him with the meat fork.

"You're a bad man!" She licked her fingers, stirring something on the stove. "It's almost ready, except I forgot to make the cranberry sauce yesterday so I guess we're going to have to eat it warm."

"It will be like cranberry dessert," Doc said.

"Hey, you could have just opened a can and plopped it out onto a plate like my mom does." I couldn't resist—I peeked into the envelope and when I saw what was in it, my breath stopped. "No way. Oh my God. No way!"

"Yes way." Carrie smiled over at me, sliding the pot off the heat to the middle of the stove. "I don't want you here all by yourself for Christmas break."

I pulled the tickets out of the envelope. "Key West?" I squeaked.

They'd been talking about taking me with them for weeks, once they found out I'd been boycotting holidays with my family all year and had no intention of doing Christmas with my mother and stepfather. Carrie said she didn't want me to be alone for the holidays. Admittedly, my first Christmas without Isabella had been pretty bad, but I figured I could get through this one without too much trauma—with some Chinese food and Blockbuster videos.

"That's depressing," Carrie said when I told her. I think she had planned this little Thanksgiving more for me than anyone when she found out that Doc couldn't get enough time off to fly back to Boston where his family lived.

"Okay, come and get it!" Carrie called. "Grab a plate and load 'er up!"

We did, taking big heaping helpings of food and sitting down at our makeshift table. None of us were very religious, but Carrie asked we bow our heads and say one thing we were thankful for.

"My girls," Doc said, looking between the two of us.

Carrie smiled at him. "Family."

"Love," I said. What else was there?

And then we ate.

She'd gone all out—a huge, gorgeous turkey, stuffing, mashed potatoes, gravy, green beans that put the mushroom soup kind my mother made to shame, none of it from a box or a can. She'd even made her own homemade cranberry sauce, which was actually the best part. It was still warm, like a sweet cranberry compote, and I had three helpings of the stuff.

Doc kept filling my wine glass and his own, but Carrie refused, drinking cranberry juice instead.

"How apropos," I noted with a laugh. "You know you are a true domestic goddess, right?" I leaned back and held my bursting stomach. I'd planned for this and had worn a skirt with elastic, not a zipper.

She smiled and took a sip of her juice. "I like to do stuff like this."

"I know it sounds caveman of me." Doc leaned over and kissed her cheek. "But she's a born wife and mother."

She flushed a deeper shade of red and looked pleased. "I never had a mother, so I don't know."

"You're not lacking for it. You mother everyone and everything." I laughed as she fed Jezebel a piece of turkey from her own plate. The cat had put on weight since we'd moved in. So had I. We all had. Carrie cared for all of us very well, in spite of her own lack of care growing up in the foster care system—or maybe because of it.

"Maybe I'll get the opportunity to be a real mother someday," she said as she started to clear our plates. Doc and I exchanged glances, and I think we both felt the pain emanating from her.

"You *are* a real mother." I clutched her wrist, holding her as she reached for my plate. I'd doubted it too often myself—how could I be a real mother if I didn't have a living baby? Our eyes met and I saw tears in hers and knew she'd understood.

"Who wants dessert?" She took my plate and headed to the kitchen. "I've got caramel apple pie and ice cream or pumpkin cheesecake."

"Homemade, of course," Doc added. He was looking at me in a way I hadn't experienced before and I wondered what he was thinking about the exchange that had just taken place.

I groaned. "I'm going to pop!"

"It's only once a year," she reminded me, putting our plates in the sink and reaching up in the cupboard for dessert ones.

"And there's always room for pie!" Doc added.

I laughed. "I thought that was Jell-O?"

After we all had a piece of each—because who could decide?—Doc made Carrie sit down so he could clean up. She protested, but he insisted and I helped him while she curled up on the couch under the blanket and watched the Macy's Thanksgiving Day Parade. Carrie had popped a VHS tape in early that morning because she was too busy cooking.

"I watch it every year," she told me, rewinding the tape. "It's a tradition. I love the floats."

Doc did the dishes and I dried and put them away. Then it was time to tackle the food.

"This turkey is enormous!" I felt like I'd been stuffing it into Tupperware for hours as Doc carved the rest of it off the carcass.

"We'll be eating turkey sandwiches until Christmas," he agreed, setting aside the wishbone and bagging the rest of the bird before washing his hands. Jezebel mewed a protest seeing all that good turkey on the carcass going into the garbage while I put the leftovers in the fridge.

"Looks like someone succumbed to the Thanksgiving tryptophan," I observed, glancing around the corner to see Carrie curled up and sleeping on the sofa.

Doc smiled fondly at her, going over to tuck the blanket up to her chin. "That's what happens when you get up at five in the morning to cook a twelve pound turkey."

"A twelve pound turkey for three people!" I exclaimed, shaking my head. "She could have bought a pre-cooked Butterball and been done with it!"

"Not my girl." He brushed her hair away from her cheek. She was angelic when she was sleeping. "She doesn't do anything halfway."

Watching him with her, seeing how much he loved her, gave me a lump in my throat. "So, about this Key West thing..." I started to change the subject.

"You're coming and that's final," Doc said firmly, taking the tablecloth off the TV trays and putting them away.

"Is that so?" I picked up my glass of wine from the kitchen counter, hiding my smile behind it. "And what are you going to do if I say no?"

"Spank you," he replied promptly, putting the TV trays in their stand. "Besides, I miss seeing both of you in bikinis. You wouldn't deprive me, would you?"

"Spank me, huh?" I raised an eyebrow.

He pushed "stop" on the remote and turned off the TV, turning to see the grin on my face. His eyes got a mischievous glint as he crossed the room toward me.

"So are you going to argue about it?" he inquired, slipping an arm around my waist and pulling me near. I moved my wine out of the way so we could be even closer.

"I just might," I breathed.

"Bad girl." He kissed me and I let him, his tongue probing, seeking entrance. He had me pressed against the counter and I felt him growing hard against my leg so I slipped my hand down to squeeze him through his jeans.

"I may just spank you for the hell of it," he gasped when our kiss broke, his eyes dark with lust.

"Promises, promises."

"Brat." He slid a hand up under my skirt, parting my thighs, and I spread for him, my eyes half-closing in pleasure as he pushed my panties aside to feel me. "So wet already. You *are* bad."

"So spank me."

He glanced over at Carrie, still sleeping on the couch. We'd been together plenty of times, the three of us, but Doc and I had never done this—not alone.

"I want you." He kissed me again, sucking at my tongue, making me moan into his mouth. "Now. Here."

"Here?" I squeaked, looking at the bedroom door just a few feet away, and then at Carrie, snoring gently under a blanket.

"Yeah." He grabbed my hips and shoved me up onto the counter. Thankfully, all the dishes were done and put away, so it was now clear. Pushing my knees back, he pulled my panties aside and leaned in, burying his face against my wetness. "Oh God, you taste so good."

"Mmmm," was all I could manage as his tongue made fat, lazy circles around my clit. I reclined as best I could, back on my elbows, putting my feet on his shoulders as he worked his mouth against my pussy. When I looked down between my thighs, I could see he had his cock out, his hand moving slowly up and down the shaft.

"Doc," I whispered, my eyes closing, hips rocking in rhythm with his tongue. "Oh Doc, you're gonna make me come."

"Good girl," he whispered back, focusing his attention back between my trembling thighs. I arched and gave a short, strangled cry, too aware that Carrie was just over there on the couch and could wake up and find us like this. But I couldn't stop. My climax was hot and fast, my pussy clamping down hard on nothing and begging for more. I wanted his cock. I needed it.

I sat up and pulled his face to mine, sucking and licking my pussy juices off his lips and tongue. He groaned and let me take his cock in my hand, stroking him against my hip and thigh as we writhed together, his hands gripping my ass, pulling me as close as he could manage.

"Should we be doing this?" I whispered against his ear, wrapping my legs around his waist. I might have been able to stop if he had said no. Maybe. God knows I didn't want to. And neither did he.

"I don't know." He hesitated, his breath hot against my neck. "But I don't care."

I don't know. Well, that was good enough. Wasn't it?

"Let's go to bed." I slid off the counter and he held me close the whole way, giving me another hard, fast kiss before pulling me into the bedroom. He closed the door behind us and that act made my heart beat faster. Carrie was out there, and her husband had just put a closed door between us.

"Now." He turned to me, not whispering anymore. "About that spanking..."

"No!" I squealed when he came after me, laughing as he tackled me onto the bed on my belly, his cock a steel rod against my ass. I took his full weight, gasping, struggling, still giggling when he clasped my wrists and pressed them to the bed.

"You're a bad girl." He nipped and licked at my neck, his voice low. "And now you're going to get your spanking."

He rolled off me and I gasped, taking deep breaths as he pulled my skirt up in the back, kneading my flesh with his hands. I squirmed when he yanked my panties down and pulled me across his lap, feeling my breath catch as his fingers probed the crack of my ass.

"Oh Doc..." I lifted my hips as his thumb moved down my wet slit.

"You like that?" He strummed me lightly at the top of my cleft.

"Mmm." I arched in response.

Then his hand came down on my ass, smacking me hard.

THWAP!

I squeaked and tried to sit up, but I couldn't regain my balance. He did it again, even harder.

THWAP!

"How about that?" he asked. "Do you like that?"

"Oww!" I howled as his hand met my stinging behind, actually feeling tears prick my eyes. "Don't!"

"Then tell me what I want to hear." The light brush of his palm was a brief respite against the heated flesh of my behind.

I searched my memory, trying to remember just what I was getting the spanking for in the first place, but my brain was still too foggy from our interlude on the kitchen counter.

"I don't—"

THWAP!

I wailed, reaching back to cover my behind with my hands, trying to pull my skirt down. "Will you stop?"

I felt him chuckle. "Then tell me what I want to hear."

"I... I love you!" I blurted and he laughed.

"Well, thank you, but that's the wrong answer."

THWAP!

Now I was getting mad. "Let me go."

"Awww, I'm just having fun." His fingers moving down between my thighs, trying to apologize. "Is that better?"

I relaxed a little, still wary. "Yes..."

"Mmm, you have such a sweet pussy." He slid a finger wetly inside. "You make me want it so bad."

"Then be nice," I warned, spreading my thighs just a little to give him more room to explore.

"But being bad feels better."

THWAP!

"Hey!" I protested, wiggling in his lap again "No fair!"

"Now, are you coming to Key West with us?" His hands dug into the flesh of my ass and I felt his teeth nipping, making me squeal. "Or not?"

"Yes!" I gasped, remembering now—the tickets to Key West for Christmas break. "Yes, I'm coming! I'm coming!"

"Not yet you're not." He had me rolled onto my back and was on top of me before I could take another breath, my wrists clasped in just one of his hands. "But you will be."

"Doc," I whispered as he kissed and nuzzled my neck, sending shivers through me, making my nipples stand up under my blouse. I wanted to be naked, to feel his hot, sweaty skin against mine. "What if Carrie comes in?"

"Then she can join us," he breathed, tugging at the top button of my blouse with his teeth, forcing it to pop open. "But if I'm being honest..." He licked down the center of my chest, stopping at the obstruction of my bra. "I hope she stays asleep."

Oh God. I hadn't wanted to admit it, how much I wanted this, wanted him—all to myself.

"Me too," I whispered, swallowing as he yanked another button and I heard a soft "clink" against the wall where it flew as it popped off my blouse. It was real silk, quite expensive—Mason's parents had bought it for me last Christmas, I remembered. "Rip it open."

He gave a low growl and let go of my wrists, grabbing the top of my blouse and parting it with one quick motion. The bottom button stuck and he yanked one more time, spreading my blouse wide and looking at me in my bra.

"Leave your hands above your head," he instructed as I reached for him, my fingers moving through his thick, dark curls. I whimpered but did as he requested and he undid my bra—it was one of my few front-hook versions—using both hands to press my breasts together and bury his face between them.

"Oh!" I gasped when he pressed one of my nipples between his lips, teasing it lightly with his tongue. Then he began to trace easy circles around my areola, spending a long, agonizing time on one before moving to the other. The switch elicited another gasp from my throat, and my hands moved to his hair, pressing his mouth to me.

"Hands above your head," he warned, eyes flashing. I groaned but complied, wiggling under him as he started working on the other nipple, trying to get it as hard and wet as the first. "You have perfect breasts." He sighed, nuzzling and kissing and licking. "Your nipples are the sweetest ever."

"Ever?" I teased. "What about your wife's? I like hers better, how fat they get when they're hard..."

"No fair." He grinned, nipping a little at the side of my breast, making me jump. "We can't do comparisons when I can't observe both subjects hands-on."

"So to speak." I was a little shy when he made me lift my hips so he could take down my skirt and my panties. We'd had sex together, well, lots of times, but I didn't think he'd ever paid this close attention to my body before.

"Sorry about the stretch marks," I apologized, closing my eyes as he kissed his way down my belly. I had proudly thought, all the way through my pregnancy, that I'd escaped them completely, but then I'd discovered I had them low, underneath—where I couldn't even see when I was pregnant. There weren't many, just a few stretching toward my hips, faded now.

"Shh." His tongue dipped into my navel. "You're beautiful."

I blushed, feeling my embarrassment melt away when he pressed himself between my thighs, breathing in my scent. He slid his hands slowly under the swell of my ass and lifted me to his mouth like I was ambrosia, making little noises in his throat as he explored the folds of my flesh with his tongue. I don't know how long he spent—it was forever, teasing me, taking me to the edge and pulling me back, again, again, and then again.

At first I would whisper, "Close, oh so close," and he would back off, kissing my labia or slipping his tongue down to probe my hole. Then I stopped saying it, but he grew wise, knowing the tell-tale tense and tremble of my thighs, the curling of my toes, all meant I was close, and he'd slow down again, making me wait. And wait. And wait.

"Please," I begged, starting to reach for him and then remembering, keeping my hands above my head. "Oh Doc, don't tease me anymore."

He lifted his head quickly, eyes bright, face full of my wetness. "No more?"

"Please," I croaked.

"Okay." He crawled up my body, poised above me, the muscles in his upper arms flexed as he held his weight off my body. "No more."

"No!" I whimpered. "Don't stop!"

"How about we do this instead?" he whispered, nudging my thighs open slightly with his and pressing his cock against my hole—perfect aim. Just a slight tilt of my hips and he would be inside.

"Don't move." He used one hand to grab my wrists, my hands still obediently clasped above my head, and held them there. "I'm going to fuck you until you come all over my cock."

I moaned softly, biting my lip to keep from crying out when he shifted his hips and plunged himself into my depths. He gave a low grunt, taking a deep breath before starting to move, his pelvis grinding against mine. He was just moving his hips, working the shaft of his cock in short, fast strokes into my pussy. My breath matched his and I started to meet him, unable to stop the motion, rocking to his rhythmic beat.

I had waited so long, teetering on the edge of climax, that my pussy was actually throbbing around his cock, a thick pulse, as he pushed me toward that precipice with relentless, deliberate assault. I bucked and buried my face in his neck, raking my teeth over his shoulder, unable to do anything with my hands because he held them still, high above my head, helpless in my own pleasure, trying not to scream as I came. My orgasm hit so hard and hot and fast it was like a lightning strike, a hot surge of illuminated ecstasy followed by a slow burn that shook my whole body like thunder.

Doc let it tremble us both, slowing his strokes and then holding still, riding out the storm of my climax with breathless wonder. And then he pulled quickly out of me, grabbing my hips and burying his face between my legs with wild abandon. I squealed and tried to roll away, my clit too sensitive for that kind of stimulation so soon, but he wouldn't let me go, his face thrashing against my pussy, driving me onward.

"No, no, no," I whispered, digging my heels into the bed, still trying to escape, but he was too strong, too determined. "Oh God, no!" His finger moved down my slit, past the hole he'd just been fucking, to the tight pucker of my ass. "Oh please, no!" I begged, giving up on keeping my hands above my head and pushing at his head, his shoulders.

But Doc wasn't taking 'no,' for an answer.

"Nooo!" I wailed, finally giving into the sensation, my clit responding in spite of my protest, my pussy and ass clenching tight. His finger was in my ass now, all the way in, fucking me hard, harder. "Oh God! Oh! Oh! Fuck! You're gonna—oh!"

He persisted, fucking my ass and licking me to yet another orgasm, and I closed my eyes against the shame of my asshole fluttering around his pumping finger as I came against his mouth and tongue.

"Now that's what I'm talking about." He moved up to kiss me, letting me taste myself on his lips and tongue. "I'm gonna fuck you so hard..."

That was all the warning I got before I was rolled over onto my belly, his cock impaling me from behind.

Not in my ass—thank God, I was afraid for a moment, trembling like a rabbit as he fumbled his cock down my crack—but plunging into my pussy, pounding me into the bed.

"Play with yourself," he panted, grabbing my hips and pulling me up to my knees. "Finger that pussy. Make yourself come again for me."

"I can't!" I protested, doing what he asked anyway, half-heartedly rubbing my pussy lips with my palm. My labia was shockingly swollen and slick, almost numb from so much pleasure.

"I'm not going to stop fucking you until you come." He grunted and drove himself in hard. "I can do this all night long."

I smirked. "Promises, promises."

"Is that a challenge?" He shoved in, balls deep, and drew out again all the way to the tip. Then he did it again. And again. The long strokes were a tease and he knew it.

"Okay," I panted, my fingers finding the aching nub of my clit. "Okay, okay. I'll come for you."

"That's my girl." He gave me the short, hard strokes again, the ones that jarred my bones and drove me against the bed and made me beg for more.

"More!" I grunted, tilting my hips so he could get just a little more bruising depth. "Oh God, give it to me! Gimme that fucking cock until I come!"

He gave a low, guttural cry at my words, his hands gripping my hips and grinding hard. I knew that sound—he was going to come. And so was I.

"Doc!" I closed my eyes and called out his name, my fingers doing the impossible and taking me over again—again! His cock pulsed once, twice, three times, oh God, I felt every surge of his cum rising up his shaft and emptying into my spasming cunt.

"Jeeeeezus," he breathed, pulling out of me with a low groan. I turned and reached for him, letting him spoon me and tug the covers up over our sweaty skin. His fingertips traced lightly over my shoulder and side, making me shiver. We were quiet, letting our breath come back to some semblance of normal, our hearts slowing to a more steady beat.

"Hey." He leaned over and kissed my temple. "I have a weird question for you."

"Hmm?" I closed my eyes and wiggled my bottom into the saddle of his hips.

"What happens... if your IUD fails?"

I startled, my eyes flying open. "It's unlikely." I'd had an IUD since Isabella was born—I wouldn't risk having another baby with Mason. I'd told Carrie about my method of birth control, and obviously she'd told Doc.

"But it could happen," he said. "Theoretically."

"Anything's possible." I reached over and picked up the thermometer off the night table next to their bed. Carrie woke up every morning to take her temperature, so hopeful. "I keep hoping to see a positive pregnancy test around instead of a thermometer."

"You and me both." He sighed. "You know, I want kids, but Carrie... she *really* wants kids. Not a million of them or anything. Just a boy and a girl—the usual matching set."

I smiled, putting the thermometer back. "That doesn't seem like too much to ask."

"If I could do it for her I would," he said softly. I turned in his arms so our bellies were pressed together.

"So would I." Our eyes met and it was like a light bulb went off in both our heads at the same time.

Doc held up his hands, shaking his head. "I didn't mean that. You can't... I would *never* ask..."

"No," I murmured. "You wouldn't ask. But I could offer."

He gaped at me. "That's too much."

"Does she have her heart set on having her own biological child?" I asked.

"She comes from foster care," he reminded me. "She knows how many babies are out there who need families." He rolled to his back, hands behind his head, looking up at the ceiling. "We've talked about adoption. I think it would be best, something like that. Pregnancy doesn't seem to agree with her. We just don't have the money now to do it. After my residency, maybe..."

"And there's no medical reason for the miscarriages?" I sat up on my elbow, looking at him.

"Not one they can find." He turned his sad eyes toward me. "Hell, I'm a doctor and even I know what we do isn't an exact science. People like to think it is, that we know everything, but the reality is we know very little, still, about the way our bodies work."

"Oh, I think I have a pretty good idea how they work..." I teased, letting my fingers walk across his chest. He smiled, clasping my hand and kissing my palm. I sat up, excited by my idea. "So, do you think she'd agree to let me carry your baby?"

He stared at me. "My baby... as in... yours and mine?"

I nodded. The thought was both terrifying and exhilarating. Part of me was screaming, *What are you thinking?* and another part of me was so joyful at the thought of being pregnant again I could barely contain myself.

"But you couldn't." He put a hand on my thigh, rubbing gently. "I mean, after what happened..."

"You mean Isabella?"

He nodded, wincing. I think Carrie was the only person I knew who didn't want to turn away when I said her name out loud.

"I don't know," I mused. "Let me think about it. Mason wanted to have another right away, but I couldn't do that. It wouldn't have been the responsible thing to do—of course, it wasn't responsible to have Isabella in the first place, but I couldn't make any other decision. Maybe it would even be healing for me to have a... a living baby."

For some reason, the thought made me very happy. They'd both given me so much—what if I could give something back to them?

"But you would have to give it up," he reminded me gently.

I shook my head. "It wouldn't be the same. I'd be giving her to you, not a stranger."

"It would be an incredible gift," he admitted, and I thought I saw tears in his eyes. "But I couldn't ask you to do it."

"You don't have to ask." I stretched out beside him again, putting my head on his chest. "I'm offering."

He took a deep breath. "Let's wait a while. Maybe Carrie will get pregnant again."

Our eyes met. Getting pregnant wasn't the problem—staying pregnant was. And neither of us knew if she could handle losing yet another one. Why put her through that?

"Hey, what happened to the parade?" Carrie appeared in the doorway, rubbing her bleary eyes.

"You fell asleep." Doc smiled a welcome and patted the bed. Carrie stripped off her jeans, climbing in wearing just her t-shirt to settle between us.

"How many times did he make you come?" she asked me sleepily as I pulled up the covers.

"Four." I flushed and looked over at Doc. He was watching me with those dark eyes, looking between the two of us together in bed—"his girls."

"He's so generous." She sighed and closed her eyes, curling her hand under her chin. Doc ran a hand over the curve of her hip over the covers, tracing the dips and valleys of her body. It was hard to believe, but he wasn't done—he wanted us both. I could tell by the look in his eyes.

"Ohhh, Doc," Carrie murmured, snuggling back against him as his hand moved under the covers, heading for the apex of her thighs. I cupped her breast in my hand—she'd been in such a hurry to get into bed she was still wearing a bra—thumbing her nipple through the material. She rocked with him, making little noises, but her eyes never opened. "I'm soooo sleepy."

"Damned turkey," I sighed, hearing her breathing start to become deeper, more even.

"She was up too early." He kissed her temple, lifting his fingers to his mouth and tasting her. "Mmm. I'm hungry again. Let's get some turkey sandwiches."

I glanced at the clock—it was only eight p.m. Carrie was snoring softly and we had all night. I followed him to the kitchen.

Chapter Eight

"Are you kidding me?" I stared at the tangle of black dental floss Carrie handed me out of her suitcase. "I'm supposed to wear this in front of Doc's *parents?*"

Carrie laughed, pulling a new white bikini out of her bag. "We'll be lucky if they don't skinny dip with us."

"Ummm." I stared at her as she started to strip, pulling her t-shirt off and unsnapping her bra. "Really?"

"Really." She slipped her jeans and panties off too. "Doc's dad is a worse flirt than he is."

"Not possible." I started to strip too, still contemplating the material, or lack thereof, in the bathing suit Carrie had brought for me. She'd insisted I couldn't wear a one-piece and when I'd protested, she said, "Don't worry, I'll pick something up for you."

This was the "something," although it wasn't much of anything at all. The thong went up the crack of my ass, leaving black strings in a triangle across my lower back. The front was another non-existent triangle and I was glad we'd both gone in for a Brazilian wax the week before—even if I'd protested the whole time and whined for an hour afterward about the pain.

"I'm not so sure about this." I adjusted the top—yikes, there wasn't much of that either! I was falling out all over the place. I was wearing far less material than Carrie was, I noticed. Her white bikini was like a snowsuit compared to my micro-suit.

She looked over at me, her eyes lighting up. "Doc's going to love it."

And she was right. The look on his face when we walked out onto the beach was priceless, like a cross between a hungry wolf and a stalking lion. It made the sun feel even warmer against my skin. But it was Doc's dad, Charles—"Call me Chuck, everybody does"—who gave a low whistle from where he was cooking burgers for lunch on the grill.

"Chuck!" Doc's mother, Nan, tsked at him from the patio table where she was valiantly trying to keep paper plates from blowing away by weighing them down with ketchup and mustard and potato salad containers. "Keep your eyes in your head."

"That *is* where I keep 'em," he retorted. He flipped one of the burgers and glanced over at us, muttering, "I can see much better that way."

"It's so hot!" Nan exclaimed, fanning herself with a paper plate and taking a seat next to Doc. "Or is it just me going all menopausal?"

"No, Mom, it's hot," Doc confirmed, squinting up at the sky.

I knew Florida would be a change from Michigan weather, of course, but the heat was still a surprise. The Baumgartners said it would be shorts weather—seventy degrees or so—but it was unseasonably warm for December, the temperature hovering in the mid-eighties all week, and we were taking full advantage of it.

"Do me." Carrie handed over a bottle of coconut scented oil and rolled onto her belly, adjusting herself on the blanket.

"I'll do you," Doc called and his father chuckled, flipping another burger.

"Like father, like son." Nan reached over and smacked Doc over the head with the paper plate, which of course didn't do much damage.

I just ignored him and rubbed stuff into Carrie's back and legs, undoing her straps like she asked, and then set about covering myself with oil. I'd paled considerably over the winter but it would only take a few days for my skin to brown up nicely. Carrie had spent the week before we left in a tanning booth, getting what she called a "starter tan." Although she had a head start, I was sure to outstrip her in no time, given my skin tone.

"Who wants cheese on their burger?" Chuck called and I was the only one who raised my hand. "You betcha." He winked and slapped on a slice of American, letting it melt while he took the rest of the burgers off the grill. They smelled so good it made my mouth water. "Soup's on! Come and get it!"

We ate a leisurely lunch, soaking up the sun, covering profound conversational topics like the weather—in Michigan, Boston and Florida—with Doc's parents. They were nice people, clearly enamored with their only son and his wife, and I liked them both, but it was still a little uncomfortable sitting nearly naked next to people who were practically strangers.

I was glad when they both went in to take an "old person nap," Chuck said with a wink, although I wondered when I saw him grab her ass on the way through the door into the house, if sleeping was all they were going to be doing.

Not that we were any better. The minute they went in, Doc was rubbing more oil into my ass while I stretched out on my belly next to Carrie on the blanket, letting his fingers slip between the crack, tugging at the little string of material there.

"Are you going to let me have it?" he leaned over to whisper.

"Stop." I shivered, feeling his finger probing the tight clench of my asshole. With all the oil, there wasn't much resistance, even though I tried. "You're bad."

"I know." He probed a little further, making me moan. "But it would feel sooo good."

I glanced around the beach, knowing there was no one around—it was totally private—but what if his parents were watching from the window or something? I flushed with embarrassment, feeling his finger wiggling, wondering what his cock might feel like there.

"Maybe," I said, mostly just to placate him, nudging his arm away. "Later."

"Promises, promises." His hand was back, this time petting me gently between the legs, making me squirm and open my thighs a little more. "God, this suit is something else. I can't resist you in it."

"Carrie picked it out." I glanced over to see she had her eyes closed, her sun hat covering her head to shade it. She was sleeping.

"Remind me to thank her profusely." His oiled fingers moved between my smooth pussy lips, making me gasp. "Oh Dani, you're wet."

"All that oil," I mumbled, biting my lip when his fingers moved to my clit.

"Nuh-uh." He made wet little circles. He knew I loved that. "That's not oil, that's you. You're turned on. I think you like parading around wearing next to nothing."

"I do not." I lifted my hips in spite of my protest, sighing with pleasure as he rubbed my clit. "It's embarrassing."

"That's probably what turns you on about it." He chuckled. "I wonder what my parents would say if they knew I was doing this."

"Your mother would hit you over the head with a paper plate again," I teased.

"I'm such a bad boy."

I gave a delighted sigh, spreading a little wider. "You are."

"But you like me that way."

"I do." I moaned against the blanket. "Faster."

"Like that?"

My clit pulsed against his fingers. "Oh yeah."

"Are you going to come for me?"

"Yes," I breathed, my face hot, my body even hotter.

"Right here in front of everybody?"

I looked up, a jolt of shame going through me, sending little lightning bolts down between my legs. "There's nobody watching."

He leaned close, his breath hot against my ear. "I'm watching."

"Oh God, I'm coming." My pussy contracted, fluttering with exquisite tightness and release, a fiery butterfly.

"Good girl." He licked his fingers.

"Doc, do you know where the aloe is?" Nan poked her head out the door and I jumped, my eyes going wide. "Your father got too much sun on his bald little head. I told him to wear a hat."

"I have some in my overnight bag," he replied. "It's on my dresser upstairs."

"Thank you." She waggled her fingers at us and we waggled ours back. Doc's still had my come on them. "You kids have fun!"

"Oh my God." I buried my face in the blanket.

Doc laughed. "I'm going for a swim. Want to come?"

I glanced at Carrie, still sleeping. "Nah. I gotta catch up with Miss Coppertone over there."

He slapped my ass as he stood and then took his shirt off, dropping it next to the blanket before taking off running toward the water. I couldn't help turning to admire him as he went. I heard him whoop when he hit the water. *Must be cold,* was my last thought before I drifted off next to Carrie, joining her in sleep.

"You have to see this tub." Carrie led me upstairs by the hand, still hot and oily and sleepy from our nap on the sand. Doc and his dad were already showered and dressed and ready for dinner, sitting on the patio and playing a game of chess.

"They're fanatics," Nan had told me, shaking her head. "This could go on for hours."

I certainly hoped not—I was hungry. Carrie and I had dozed most of the afternoon away, sleeping the jetlag off, both of us growing browner by the minute. When Doc had woken me to say it was dinner time, I couldn't believe it.

"Wow," I whispered as Carrie opened the bathroom door, revealing an enormous black marble bathtub with a shower stall beside it. "That can't be real. It's like a hotel."

"I know." She clapped her hands like an excited little kid, shutting the door behind her and going over to start the water running. "I've been dying to share this with somebody."

"Do we have time?" I was already stripping down, tossing my suit, such as it was, into the sink and sitting next to Carrie on the edge of the tub.

Carrie snorted. "We're girls. We can take as long as we want. Besides, when Doc and his dad play chess, it takes *forever.*"

We let the water run, swinging our feet over the side until it was full. Carrie poured lavender bubble bath in and a fine sheen of bubbles started forming at the surface as we slid into the water.

"Oh God," I groaned, settling myself beside her, leaning against the slanted back of the tub. There was plenty of room for both of us to sit side by side, our hips rubbing. "This is heaven!"

"Tell me about it." She leaned over and pressed a button on the side and the Jacuzzi jets started up, giving us both a heated massage. The bubbles started to rise around us, covering the surface of the water and we played in them, blowing them around.

"Look, a bubble dress." I stood, water sheeting off my body, leaving a lacy trail of bubbles all over my body.

"Damn." Carrie's eyes were bright. "That's the sexiest dress I've ever seen on you."

"Let's see yours."

She stood too and I glanced over to the mirror, seeing two very shapely women covered in foam. Carrie took a step toward me, sliding her arms around my waist and resting her cheek against my soapy shoulder. I closed my eyes, feeling the soft press of her breasts and sweetly rounded belly against mine as we kissed.

"I want to show you something," she whispered, taking a step back and sinking fully down into the water. I watched, bemused, as she hung onto the tub and put her feet up over the edge. She leaned back a little, parting her knees, the bubbles obscuring her body.

"What—?" I blinked as she moaned and started rocking, making waves in the water. And then I understood—she had positioned herself over one of the jets and was letting the water pulse against her clit.

She opened her eyes, a little breathless. "Wanna try?"

"Hell yeah." I got down into the water, situating myself beside her in the tub and finding a jet to ride. "Oh! Fuck!"

"Mmmm-hmmm," she agreed, closing her eyes again and rolling her hips. "Get it right on your clit..."

The pulse was rapid-fire against my pussy, different from a tongue or even Carrie's vibrator. The water was soft and hard at the same time, kissing my clit with a steady, pulsing stream of heat. I lost myself almost immediately, moaning and trying to get even closer to the sensation.

"Ride it," Carrie whispered, her eyes still closed, her mouth a little open with her pleasure. "Oh yeahhhh I'm gonna come!"

I watched it happen, her breasts floating in the water, nipples hard and poking through the bubbles, her back arched, hands gripping the edge with white knuckles. Her orgasm made me want mine even more.

"Oh Carrie," I gasped, splaying my thighs wider and nudging my clit against the delicious, hot rush of water. I chased my climax in circles, divine spirals that ended in infinity, my whole body bucking with my orgasm. I shuddered, letting myself go and nearly drowning as I sank into the tub, coming up sputtering and covered in bubbles.

Carrie laughed and I did too, spitting out soapy water and wiping at my eyes. She used a washcloth to clean off my face.

"Want to do it again?" she asked, grinning.

"Hell yeah!"

The knock on the door startled us both. "Girls?" It was Nan. I bit my lip, trying not to laugh. "Are you all right in there?"

"We're fine!" Carrie called. "Just getting ready! Give us five minutes!"

"Hurry girls!" She sighed, moving away from the door. "I'm hungry!"

"Me too," Carrie reached over to cup my still spasming pussy and I moaned. "I can't wait to eat..."

"Bad!" I grinned and pushed her probing fingers away. "Come on, we better wash. Your husband and your in-laws are waiting."

"Okay, fine." She sighed, reaching across the tub for the shampoo. "Dinner first. Eat later."

We both giggled and started to wash our hair.

It was dark when Carrie slipped in my room, shaking me awake and whispering, "We're going skinny-dipping," into my ear. I came awake slowly, not sure if she was real or part of my dream. When I felt her hand slip under the covers, cupping my breast and thumbing my nipple, I knew she was definitely real.

"Come on." She kissed me in the dark, her lips soft and warm. "Doc's waiting."

"Well we can't have that." I smiled sleepily and followed her out into the hallway and down the stairs.

Thankfully they were carpeted and we had bare feet so we made a minimal amount of noise. I didn't think Doc's parents would care that we were going skinny dipping at midnight—but I didn't exactly want them seeing or, God forbid, joining us.

"Ready?" Doc looked up as Carrie opened the back door and led me out onto the beach. The night air was cool and when I looked up there was a full moon and an infinite number of stars above our heads.

"Not quite." Carrie pulled her t-shirt off over her head and dropped it on the sand, revealing her nude body underneath. "Now I'm ready."

"Mmm." Doc stood, sliding his boxers down and stepping out of them. He was half-hard just watching his wife walk toward the water.

I shivered, still half-asleep. "Is it cold?"

"I'll keep you warm." He held out his hand and I pulled my t-shirt off too, leaving it on the sand along with my panties as we walked toward the edge of the water. Carrie was already wading in, her body full and lush in the moonlight, a goddess in sea foam, Venus in reverse.

"Oooo cold!" I protested, stopping at the water's edge as the waves rushed over my feet.

"Oh come on," Carrie called over her shoulder. "We're from Michigan. This is bath water compared to Lake Superior!"

"Well, that's true," I admitted, watching Doc wade out to catch up to his wife. Still I didn't move. "Are there sharks?" I called.

"Come on, you baby!" Carrie laughed. "Or I'm going to keep him all to myself." She turned and threw her arms around Doc's neck, wrapping her legs around his waist. He took her weight, laughing and sinking down into the waves, taking her with him. I watched them playing for a moment, leaping through the water like dolphins, the moonlight making the whitecaps look like diamonds.

I waded slowly out, letting myself gradually get used to the water temperature. Doc and Carrie were kissing, her arms and legs wrapped around him. I got brave and dove under the waves, slicking my hair back as I came up beside them.

"There she is." Carrie turned and held a hand out to me. "Isn't it awesome?"

"It's beautiful." I wasn't looking at the water or the sky or the beach in the moonlight. I was looking at her.

"Come here, girl." Doc shifted Carrie to his hip and reached for me, taking my weight on the other side. We both wrapped our arms and legs around him, clinging to each other and rocking with the waves. I could feel his cock against my leg, hard under the water, and then Carrie's hand reaching down to caress him. He groaned and thrust up into her fist, rocking all of us.

I turned his face to me and kissed him, sucking at his tongue, licking the salt water off his lips. His hands were full of both of us and he squeezed my ass, gripping me tight.

"I want your cock," Carrie whispered in his ear, working her way around the front of him, climbing him like a tree. He tried to juggle me too, but lost his grip and I fell into the water, coming up with a mouth full of salt.

"Okay, girls, this way," Doc directed, laughing at me as I waded toward shore looking like a drowned rat. We made it to the beach, kneeling together in the wet sand at the water's edge, the three of us pressed together in the cool night air. Carrie had her hand wrapped around his cock again and I was kissing him, letting him fondle and play with my breasts at his leisure.

"Bend over." Doc turned his wife around on her knees and she put her ass up for him, rounded globes of flesh in the moonlight.

"What about me?" I pouted, already guiding his cock toward her pussy, although I think he knew the way, even in the dark.

"You're next." He captured my mouth with his, sucking at my tongue as he began to fuck her. The force of him drove her forward and she moaned softly, digging her palms into the wet sand for purchase and shoving her ass back against the thrust of his cock. I slid my hand down to cup my mound as I watched them, seeing the wet pull of his dick as he slid out and then back into her cunt. I wanted it—I wanted his cock, I wanted her pussy. I wanted them both.

"Poor Dani," Doc whispered, glancing over to see me touching myself. "Soon."

"Promises, promises." I sighed, reclining back on the wet sand next to his wife and fingering my pussy. Carrie leaned over and kissed my mouth, her lips salty, her tongue hot against mine. "Does it feel good?" I asked, watching her face, seeing the twist and pull of pleasure crossing her features.

"Fuck yeah," she panted, her eyes half-closed, her mouth making a little "o" as he slammed into her again and again. "Oh God. Oh Doc. Oh!"

I saw her orgasm come over her face, the way her brow furrowed and her nose wrinkled, the sweet tug of her lower lip under her teeth. She hardly made a sound, but I knew she was coming all over his cock, squeezing it with every hard clench of her cunt, trying to milk him of his cum.

"Meeee too," I begged, my fingers pumping into my pussy, faster, harder, aching for more. "Doc, please, fuck me too."

He swallowed and gasped, gripping his wife's hips as she slid forward and collapsed onto the sand beside me. Then he moved between my legs, spreading them wide and back. I held my knees, waiting for the hard plunge of his dick, begging him for it, pleading with my mouth, my eyes, my hands, my pussy.

"Yes!" I cried as he shifted his weight and took me, the slick thrust of his cock like a gift. I thanked him for it with every movement, my nails raking over the hard, flat planes of his belly, my pussy squeezing his length. Carrie rolled toward me and sucked my nipple into her mouth, making me arch in the wet sand.

"That's a good girl," she murmured against my breast, licking my nipple as if it was a little clit. "Take that fucking cock. Does that feel good? You like him fucking you?"

"Yes!" I panted, planting my heels in the sand and lifting my hips to meet his hard thrusts. "Yes! Yes! Yes!"

"Does it make you want to come?" she purred, and I saw that she was playing too, her fingers lost in the wetness of her cunt.

"Let me lick you." I reached for her in the moonlight and she settled herself over my face, her belly toward Doc's, watching him fuck me.

"Oh Dani," she moaned, rocking her hips as I parted her slippery labia with my tongue, searching valiantly for her tiny clit. "Oh baby, that's so fucking good!"

I grabbed her ass in my hands, giving her a tongue lashing as Doc slammed me against the sand, his cock throbbing between my legs. He felt impossibly huge, as if he could fill me completely.

Carrie wiggled on my face and I heard soft slapping sounds. Then she squealed and moaned. "Oh yeah, Doc, slap my tits. Hard—harder!"

Her hands gripped my breasts in the dark, squeezing and twisting my nipples. I gave a muffled cry against her pussy, but no one could hear it. I was drowning in her cunt, flooded with her, and all I wanted was more, more.

"Oh fuck," Doc cried, his hands moving over my waist, grabbing onto my thrusting hips. "Ohhhhh fuck!"

He was going to come. I whimpered and sucked harder at Carrie's clit, grinding my hips up, meeting him. And then I felt Carrie's tongue probing between my pussy lips, her fingers spreading them open so she could delve inside.

"Oh baby," I whispered into the night, but then her pussy was rocking against my tongue again, eager, greedy. I wasn't chasing my climax anymore—it was chasing me.

"Oh God! Oh now!" She shuddered and buried her face against my pussy as Doc gave one final, guttural cry, his hips bucking against mine as he started to come. I felt every swollen throb of his shaft, the hot spasm of my pussy around his cock milking him dry.

Carrie rolled off me onto the sand, resting next to me. Breathless, I found her hand and squeezed it tight. Doc crawled up beside me and collapsed onto his belly, his cheek resting against my breast, the perfect cushion.

"Again?" I prompted, opening my eyes to the myriad of stars on black velvet above us.

Doc groaned but Carrie laughed. "Shower first," she said. "I've got sand... you don't even want to know where I've got sand."

"Should we conduct an inspection?" I grinned and slid my hand over her hip, walking my fingers toward her cleft.

"In the shower," she laughed. "But we have to be quiet. Don't want to wake the parents."

The shower was welcome heat after the cool night air. We used the downstairs shower instead of going to the big one upstairs—no one wanted to wake Doc's parents. We washed each other so thoroughly, every crack and crevice, that not a speck of sand was left.

"Inspection time," I announced, dropping to my knees in front of Carrie and running my hands up over her hips and belly and ribs. Her tummy was slightly more rounded than it had been when I met her—of course, so was mine. We were all putting on holiday weight, and I made a mental note to head back to the university gym after break.

"Find anything?" She leaned back in her husband's arms and let me part her thighs.

"Just this one thing," I breathed, inching my mouth close to her crevice. "Right here."

She moaned when I sucked her clit between my lips and Doc kissed her quiet, his soapy hands moving over her heavy breasts. She was so sexy like that, thighs spread, chest heaving, eyes closed and mouth agape, totally lost in her pleasure. The water ran down her skin in little rivulets, beading on her belly and breasts, and I licked off the streams that merged at the apex of her thighs.

"Hold me, Doc," she begged, leaning even further back against him. "Oh spread me open for her hot little mouth!"

He took her weight, lifting her legs, grabbing into her thighs and pulling them far back. It made her swollen pussy protrude into my mouth even more, her usually hidden clit stand out. I groaned and buried my face against the slippery wet swell of her cunt, focusing right on her pleasure center. But that still wasn't enough.

My pussy was begging for attention and I spread my own legs a little so I could touch myself while I licked her. Doc's fingers dug into the flesh of her ass and thighs, leaving red marks, but she didn't seem to care. His eyes were dark with lust as he watched me suck at his wife's pussy, and I couldn't help myself—I had to have him too.

Doc groaned when I reached for his cock, water-wet but also slick with pre-cum at the head, making it easy to stroke him. It wasn't easy to coordinate, licking, rubbing, stroking, but I caught a rhythm after a while. Carrie went first, shaking and moaning in Doc's arms. He let one of her legs down to cover her mouth with his hand and she let go then with muffled screams, begging for more and then pleading me to "stop, stop, stop!"

"Christ," Doc whispered as his wife sank to her knees beside me, the two of us turning our attention to his cock in the aftermath of her orgasm, looking up at him with wet hair and faces, eager for more. "I think I may be the luckiest man on planet earth."

"You better remember it," Carrie teased, her hand joining mine on his shaft. My mouth sought the head of his cock, greedy to be filled, and he let himself lean back against the tile as we gently fought for his dick, tongues meshing, fingers pumping.

"How could I possibly forget?" Doc gasped, his hands moving in our hair, guiding first me, then her, burying his cock in her throat and then mine, as if trying to decide which he liked best. We both did our best to please him, each working our mouths and tongue with as much skill as we could muster.

"I want your tits," Doc growled, grabbing onto mine and pressing them together. He soaped his hands up and rubbed them all over my breasts, making them extra slippery. Then he lowered his hips and pressed my flesh around his shaft, thrusting into my cleavage.

"Oh yeah," Carrie breathed, watching her husband fuck my tits. "That's hot." She was fingering herself, going for it again—God, we were all insatiable with each other. I could never get enough.

"Fuck my tits," I begged, my fingers thrust deep into my pussy, fucking my own hand like it was a cock. I wished it was. I wished he had at least two—one for her and one for me. Maybe more. One for my mouth, my pussy, my tits... my ass... oh God...

"Come all over me!" I pleaded, desperate for it. Doc moved his hips fast, his cock lost in the slippery, soapy press of my flesh, his breath coming in labored pants.

"Fuuuuuuck," he whispered, his face twisting in pleasure, his pelvis grinding against my chest as the first thick rope of his cum bathed my throat. The next wave hit the top of my cleavage, dripping back down into the soapy crevice, and that's the moment that I whimpered and fully gave in to my climax.

Carrie was coming too, rocking her hips and resting her forehead against my shoulder, watching her husband flood my tits with his cum. She rubbed it into my flesh like lotion with her other hand, slicking me up nicely before we all stood, washing off the mess again.

When we snuck back to bed—Doc and Carrie to their room with the double bed and me to mine with the little twin—I couldn't help it, I touched myself one more time before I could fall asleep, finally almost-satisfied, remembering the weight of them on me, in me, loving me.

Chapter Nine

I woke up in Doc and Carrie's bed on the morning we were supposed to fly home from Key West, not quite sure where I was. I vaguely remembered drinking margaritas the night before—Chuck mixed them a lot stronger than Doc did—and dancing out on the patio with Carrie. Doc's parents went to bed at midnight and left us out on the beach alone. Carrie had passed on the margaritas, saying her stomach was a little upset, but it didn't stop her from grinding with me until two in the morning, with Doc occasionally joining us so we could sandwich him between our writhing bodies.

I was half out of the bed, my arm dangling to the floor, one leg off the edge, and when I turned my head, I saw Carrie sleeping soundly, a little drool leaking out onto her pillow, her hair mussed around her face. On the other side of her, Doc had his cock in his fist, hand moving up and down the shaft, his breath a light pant. His motion shook the bed a little and I realized that's what had woken me. I wasn't in my bed, I was in theirs, and as I listened to Doc stroking his cock, I remembered just exactly what we'd been doing the night before.

He shifted his hips and murmured something, clearly lost in a fantasy. Who was he picturing, I wondered, me or his wife? Or both of us? And what deliciously deviant thing was he doing to us in his imagination? I didn't want to wake up Carrie, she was sleeping so sweetly, but my pussy starting asking for attention as I listened to Doc. I tried to do it as quietly as I could, sneaking my hand slowly down under my panties. I was amazed I was actually still wearing a pair, after the night before.

"Oh yeah, Dani, give me that sweet little ass," Doc murmured, giving a low groan. "Fuck, that's so *tight.*"

I saw him lick the circle of his thumb and forefinger and slide it slowly over the head of his dick and knew now just what he was imagining. My ass clenched in response, but my fingers moved in faster circles against my swollen clit.

He was really shaking the bed now and when I glanced at Carrie I saw her eyes were open and she had a sleepy smile on her face. She was listening too. I met her eyes as he imagined fucking my ass, thrusting up into his own fist, and she winked at me.

"Are you sure you don't want the real thing?" Carrie purred, turning over and surprising the hell out of him. He gave a little yelp but there was nowhere to go—he was decidedly caught. Aside from his initial surprise, he didn't mind at all when she reached for his cock and took up where he had left off. "You want to fuck Dani's tight little asshole?"

I squeaked in protest at her offering me up as a sacrificial lamb, but my body responded in spite of my mental denial. My ass clenched again in fear, though, as I imagined it. God, he was so *big.* How was it possible? Although I'd seen it happen, I'd watched Carrie take him that way, and she didn't cry or scream or tell him to stop—in fact, quite the opposite.

"What do you say, Dani?" Carrie's hand moved over the slope of my shoulder into the small of my back. "You ready for that?"

I bit my lip, my tummy tight, nipples hard with excitement. Was anyone ever really ready for anything? "No," I whispered, swallowing hard. "But I want to anyway."

"That's a good girl." Carrie smiled as she petted my behind, making me arch into her hand like a cat. "But you have to be quiet as a mouse. Can you do that?"

She glanced toward the door and I looked at it, too, in the early morning light seeping through the blinds. We had locked it last night for a little extra privacy, but Doc's parents were on the other side and had no idea all three of us were in here doing very naughty things—and contemplating even more twisted ones.

"I'll try," I whispered back. Doc groaned at my assent, the look of hunger in his eyes so powerful it made me tremble.

"Let me get her ready for you, baby." Carrie turned me and I followed her non-verbal instruction, rolling to my back and spreading my thighs. I was surprised by the position, sure that I would have to be on my hands and knees, my face buried into a pillow, red with shame.

And I was also sure she was going to reach over into the drawer where she'd put the KY and just lube me up for him. I tensed, waiting, but she settled herself between my thighs, kissing my swollen labia, her tongue parting my cleft from top to bottom, once, twice, again. It was a tease, a slow burn, making me close my eyes so I could fully experience and relish the feeling.

When her tongue started inching lower with every pass, I noticed but didn't mind, feeling her probe into my slick hole before starting at the top of my cleft again and sliding her way down, going a little further every time. First it was my hole, then it was her tongue lashing over my perineum, down and down until she reached the first wrinkle of my asshole. I tightened briefly, but her tongue reset at the top again and the next time she traced the same distance, plus just a little bit more. And then a little bit more. I would tense at first and then relax, contract and release, growing more and more used to the feel of her tongue probing the furrow of my ass.

Beside me, Doc had his cock ready in hand, but he wasn't stroking it. Instead he just watched his wife's ministrations with a ravenous gaze, the swell of his dick showing all of us just how hungry he was. But Carrie wasn't done. She made one more pass down my crevice, stopping and probing at her final destination, her fingers collecting my juices and then making lazy circles around my clit.

Her tongue stayed pressed against my asshole though, licking, sucking, making me flush with embarrassment, but pleasure too. I had experimented a little, let them finger my ass and play with it while we were having sex, but this was different, much more intimate—and shameful. I squirmed, fighting with the pleasure, but too consumed by it to deny it.

"That's my girl," Doc whispered, getting closer, his lips pressed against my cheek. "Let her make you come like that."

I didn't want to. Oh, but I wanted to. Her fingers were expert, rolling my clit along in just the right direction, her tongue relentless in its exploration of my crease, and I couldn't stop it if I tried. She patiently teased my orgasm out bit by glorious bit, giving me nowhere to go but up.

"Oh yes!" I arched, my moan growing with the sensation, and Doc covered my mouth with his, muffling the sound of my climax. I smothered my frenzied orgasm against his lips, frantic with ecstasy.

"She's ready for you, Doc," Carrie murmured, kneeling up between my thighs, finally reaching into the drawer for the KY.

I panted, eyes half-closed, still floating on the cloud of my climax when Doc and Carrie traded places. I looked up at him, no longer terrified but still hesitant as he let Carrie squeeze KY onto his cock and rub it in with her hand.

"I'll go easy," Doc assured me as Carrie brought my legs back, curling my bottom around. "I promise. If it hurts too much, tell me to stop and I will."

"Too much?" I gulped.

Carrie stretched out beside me, already using her tongue around my nipple to soften me up as Doc situated himself. It wasn't like I hadn't been in this position before with him—he'd fucked me this way lots of times. But now he bypassed the soft, supple stretch of my pussy to prod the snug, humid hole of my ass.

"Just relax," Carrie urged, gently rolling one nipple between her thumb and forefinger, still focusing her tongue on the other. "Let him do it."

I bit my lip as he shifted his weight forward, the slippery head of his cock meeting initial resistance, making me whimper at the sudden feeling of pressure. He hesitated, watching my face as he moved his hips a little at a time, concern mixed with lust in his eyes.

"Okay?" He pushed in a little deeper.

"Okay." I nodded, realizing I'd been holding my breath. The pressure was incredible, but there wasn't any real pain. I felt as if I was being stretched wide in ways I hadn't experienced since childbirth, although that had involved a lot more pain and unfortunately a much less happy ending.

"Easy, girl," Carrie urged as I began to struggle. He was pushing in deeper, God, he was so *huge!* I couldn't take anymore, I couldn't possibly... "Almost there."

What did that mean? I moaned and clenched and bit my lip but I didn't tell him to stop and he didn't, finally pressing past a tight band of muscle in my ass that made us both sigh in relief.

"Oh Dani." Doc swallowed, closing his eyes tight, his breathing hard as if he'd already made a great effort. "Oh my God."

"Is it in?" I tried to see but Carrie's blond head was in my way, her mouth and tongue and fingers far too busy with my breasts and nipples to stop.

"The head is," she informed me as Doc slid forward, his face showing every inch of pleasure before his pelvis met mine. And then he was all the way in. I could feel it, stretching, opening, but not hurting. The initial sensation of pain was gone. "Now he can fuck you..."

"Not for long," Doc groaned, watching his wife kneading my breasts and looking down to see his cock buried in my ass.

"That's okay," I assured him.

He chuckled. "Now that's a challenge."

"No, it isn't!" I protested as he began to thrust. Oh God, if I'd thought I could feel the size of him before, now it was tenfold, his entire length moving in and out of the tight halo of my ass. "Oh my God!"

"Now for the fun part." Carrie kissed her way down my belly and fixed her mouth over my mound. I moaned with surprise and impossible distraction, her tongue focusing its attention right at my core. Doc was taking it slow, his hands on my hips, eyes closed, lost in his own pleasure.

Then Carrie slipped two fingers into my pussy, fucking me in the same rhythm as Doc, speeding up when he did. I moaned and began to thrust back against her fingers and his cock as she slipped another finger in, three of them now pumping in and out of my cunt, both of my holes filled completely.

And her mouth was taking me places I was aching to go. I was going to come, and hard, with a cock stuffing my ass and her fingers buried in my pussy.

"Please," I whispered, frantic with need and desperate to climax. Doc fucked me hard now, slamming into my ass, and the sensation was incredible. I could barely keep my moans to whimpers, my screams to squeaks.

"Oh God, I'm gonna come, I'm gonna—" I whispered, my head thrashing from side to side as my pussy and ass clamped down tight in the first wave of my orgasm. Doc gave a low cry and arched as he thrust deep and I felt his cock pulsing with his climax. My ass began milking him involuntarily, spasming again and again, drawing every bit of his cum into my hot recesses.

"Oh Dani." His voice was shaking as he slowly pulled out of me, making me squeal and bite my lip. I went from utterly full to completely empty as Carrie withdrew her fingers. "Oh sweetheart."

Carrie came up to kiss me and I lazily tasted myself in her mouth as Doc leaned forward and collapsed against me, his cheek against my breasts.

"What a gift," he breathed, eyes still closed, breath just returning to normal.

"Merry Christmas," I announced and laughed, although Christmas Day was a week away. The Baumgartners had done presents together this week.

Nan and Chuck had even been kind enough to give me something, a very nice black cardigan—"For those cold winters," Nan informed me—but Carrie and Doc and I were waiting to exchange gifts.

"Indeed." Carrie kissed my cheek and rolled out of bed, reaching for her robe. "I'm going to take one last long bath before we go. My Christmas present to me."

Our eyes met and I knew just exactly what she was going to be doing in the bathtub. She winked at me before heading to the bathroom. I heard her lock the door before she closed it. Doc rolled to his back with a shuddering breath, but he welcomed me when I snuggled against his side.

"Speaking of Christmas gifts..." I ran my fingernail over the dark line of hair that trailed from his navel downward. "I've decided."

"Hm?" He didn't open his eyes. He was still far away.

"I'm going to have your baby."

His eyes flew open. "Dani..."

"It will be the best Christmas present we can give her." I knew it was true and so did he. I saw it in his eyes, his longing and his fear. "Please. Let's tell her when we get home."

He was quiet, his hand moving through my hair in the silence and I just waited.

Finally, he sighed. "Okay." He kissed the top of my head and hugged my hip with one hand. "I can't say no to you."

"Ditto." My tracing fingernail scratched lightly over his balls, making him groan.

"I noticed." His finger slipped between the still slick crack of my ass. "Let's do that again while my wife's in the bath."

"Doc..." I protested but his finger slipped in easily.

"I thought you couldn't say no..." he teased, starting to move it in and out of me.

I groaned. "Okay, yes. Yes."

"Was that a yes?" He rolled me onto my belly, slipping another finger in.

"Oh God yes."

Thank goodness Carrie took long baths.

<hr/>

I felt like a different person sitting across from Mason at Sweetwater. So much had changed. I couldn't help but wonder if this was the last time we would be together or see each other. It seemed impossible, but with him moving home and me—hopefully—going to Italy, it was actually quite likely.

"I got my stuff out while you were... gone." Mason stared moodily at his Coke. He didn't like talking about me living with the Baumgartners and had been really pissed off when I told him I was going with them on vacation in Key West. He hadn't even asked me if I'd had a good time, not that I'd really expected him to.

My heart thudded in my chest. "You didn't touch Isabella's room, did you?"

"No, Dani." He shook his head and sighed. "But you're going to have to move the rest of the stuff out this week. Her room too."

"I know." I blinked fast and sipped my coffee. It was too hot and I burned my tongue. "I told you I would. I will."

"So, I have this." He reached into the inside pocket of his jacket and pulled out a folded pack of papers. "Did you get your copy in the mail?"

"Yeah." Our mailbox had been stuffed full after Key West, mostly advertisements and gamer magazines. I'd been hoping for a letter from the study abroad program, but instead I'd found a letter from a lawyer containing divorce papers. "I thought you didn't want to get a divorce."

He shrugged. "I don't think there's really anything else to do now." He unfolded the papers, flipping to the last page. I saw his signature on one side, and a blank line with my name typed underneath on the other.

"Is this really it?" I asked as he handed me a pen. The top was all chewed and I had a twinge of regret. Mason always chewed his pen tops to shreds. "We can sign this thing and it's over?"

"The lawyer said it was easy when you didn't have kids."

That made me wince. I signed my name on the bottom, dated it, and handed the papers back to him. "Well. There you have it."

"There's also this." He reached back into his pocket, pulling out a folded piece of paper. "Your settlement."

I looked at the paper as he put it on the table, frowning. "My what?"

"It's so there won't be any alimony or claim to anything in the future." He cleared his throat and pushed it towards me. I stared at him, understanding immediately that this had been his parents' idea. Clearly they were afraid I would come after him at some point, somehow, for money.

"I don't want it." I'd read the divorce agreement—well most of it, anyway. I didn't really care, as long as legally we weren't married anymore once it was filed, but I didn't remember reading anything about some sort of "settlement."

"Take it." Mason sighed. "Take it and go to Italy and... be happy."

The sadness and hope mixed in his voice made me pick it up and unfold it. I stared at the number in the little box in disbelief. "This isn't right."

"Yeah it is." Mason folded the divorce papers and tucked them back into his jacket. "My parents started a retirement account for us and a... a college fund for Isabella. That's what was in it."

"Twenty thousand dollars?" I choked, my hand trembling as I held it in my hand.

"It should pay for your trip and living expenses in Italy." He looked at me over the table. "Right?"

I sat back in my seat, my breathing shallow. "I... I don't know what to say."

"I do." Mason stood, holding his hand out to me. "Goodbye."

I took his hand, but I didn't shake it. Instead, I stood, putting my arms around his waist and hugging him. He hesitated but then put his arms around me too, his grip tightening briefly before letting me go.

"Goodbye, Mason." I felt tears stinging my eyes and blinked them back. "I love you."

"I know." He kissed my cheek, picking up the check and putting it in my hand. "Better put this in a safe place."

He grinned when I tucked it under my t-shirt, into my bra. Then he turned and left without another word.

The mail I'd been hoping to find when I came home from Key West was waiting for me when I got back from signing divorce papers with Mason. I opened the envelope, standing at the mailbox, shivering with both cold and fear. I remembered opening my acceptance letter to U of M, Mason asking me over the phone, "Is it a thick envelope or a thin one?" He'd already received his acceptance. "A thick one," I'd replied and he had hooted and whooped. "That means you're in! The rejections are thin!"

This was a thin envelope. My heart dropped as I took out the letter with shaking hands, gripping the paper tightly against the wind.

Dear Ms. Danielle Stuart, we are pleased to inform you that you have been accepted...

I closed my eyes and felt the tears that had been threatening the whole walk home from Sweetwater spilling down my cheeks. *Italy. I'm going to Italy.*

I hadn't known how I was going to pay for everything, but now I had twenty thousand dollars tucked away in my bra and plenty of means to do it. I looked back at the letter in my hands, my tears dropping onto the paper, blurring some of the words, and saw the dates at the bottom: *Starting September 10...*

Math had never been my best subject—that was how I'd gotten pregnant with Isabella in the first place. I'd known, of course I had, when the program started. And how long a pregnancy lasts. Even if I got pregnant next month, I realized, I wouldn't be due until October. I'd been so excited to give them a baby, I hadn't even considered the timing. How could I possibly give the Baumgartners their dream while still living my own?

I walked slowly back to the apartment, seeing Doc's Cadillac parked in front—an unusual afternoon off. I shoved the letter into my pocket and wiped my wet face with my mittens before opening the front door. Jezebel mewed at my entrance and batted at my scarf as I unwound it and threw it over the couch, along with my coat. It was too quiet. Had they gone out?

I pulled off my boots and walked in stocking feet toward the bedroom, calling out, "Carrie?" I had the door open before I heard them, Carrie giggling and Doc laughing as they rolled around naked on the bed.

"Sorry." I took a step back, going to close the door, but Carrie held her hand out to me.

"Come join us," Doc called, pulling the edge of the sheet up and exposing Carrie's nude bottom and Doc's raging hard-on. I hesitated, feeling the weight of my divorce, my future, as I looked at them together. They had taken me in, made me their friend, their lover, had practically adopted me when it came down to it. But what was I doing here? What was I doing with my life?

"Come on, sweetness." Carrie crooked her finger at me, smiling mischievously, and I remembered just what I was doing with the Baumgartners. I didn't care of it was crazy or mixed-up or weird. I wanted it, and I wasn't going to deny myself anymore. I took off my jeans and panties and hopped into bed in my t-shirt. They moved around and made room for me in the middle.

"I'm glad you're here," Doc said as I snuggled down between them. "Carrie, Dani and I have something to tell you." He leaned over and kissed his wife's cheek. The look on his face was so loving and sweet I thought I might melt into a puddle on the bed. "Sort of a Christmas present. Right, Dani?"

I thought of the letter in the pocket of my jacket and realized—it didn't matter. It was true that Mason and I hadn't managed to fix our broken marriage after Isabella. The pieces just wouldn't go back together, no matter how hard we tried. And I regretted it. But this thing I had with the Baumgartners wasn't broken, and I wasn't about to jeopardize it. I wanted this—I wanted Doc and Carrie, this love, this life together. And I wanted to give them this gift. If I didn't, I knew I would regret it for the rest of my life. Italy could wait, but this wouldn't.

"Well, that's funny." Carrie grinned. "I have something to tell you too. The best Christmas present ever."

Doc met my gaze over his wife's glowing face and my eyes widened. Somehow I knew. I already knew.

"I'm pregnant." She could barely contain her excitement.

Doc made a sound like he'd been punched in the gut. "Are you sure?"

"More sure than I've ever been." She had tears in her eyes as she looked between us. "I've kept it to myself for so long. I'm almost four months. Sixteen weeks." She took each of our hands and pressed it against her lower belly. It was slightly rounded and even a little hard. How had I not noticed? Had I been that self-involved? And then it all fell into place—she'd been so tired, avoiding alcohol, and her weight gain didn't have anything to do with the holidays.

"*How* far along?" Doc sat straight up in bed, gaping down at her. "Jesus, I thought you were just putting on a little winter weight!"

"I used your cream, Dani," she explained. "I went back to that chiropractor and he gave me more. He said after the first trimester, I probably wouldn't need it anymore, that I would carry to term once the placenta took over production of progesterone."

"You what?" Doc blinked at her. "You went to some kind of quack?"

Carrie sighed. "I knew you'd say that. Doc, listen to me. Sixteen weeks! She's sixteen weeks!"

"She?" Doc was utterly flabbergasted. "You know it's a girl?"

"I had to." She pleaded with him for understanding, pressing her hand against her belly again. "I had to see her moving, know she was alive in there before I told you. But now I know for sure. I felt her."

"You did?" Doc ran his hands over her still rather flat belly—she had phenomenal stomach muscles, it was no wonder she was hardly showing. "You can feel her?"

"Uh huh." Carrie smiled as Doc leaned over and feathered kissed on her tummy below her navel.

"I can't believe it." Doc settled there, his cheek against her thigh, his hand petting her belly. "Baby," he whispered, his eyes bright. "Baby..."

"Are you mad?" Carrie asked, her hand in his hair.

"Are you kidding me?" He laughed.

She looked over at me for a reaction, but I was still too stunned to speak at the perfection of the moment. "So what was your present?"

I opened my mouth to speak, wondering how to phrase it now, and then just blurted it out. "I was going to offer to carry a baby for you guys."

Her eyes filled with tears. "Oh Dani."

"But now I guess I'm going to Italy."

Doc's head snapped up, his eyes wide. "You got in?"

I nodded, blinking back my own tears, too overwhelmed with it all to speak.

"Damn, we're going to have to do some big-time celebrating." Doc smiled at me and I smiled back.

"I bought something for the baby," Carrie whispered in my ear. "Just a little pink bunny. But it seemed right... like it's all going to be okay."

"It is." I kissed her cheek, feeling tears sting my eyes as I thought of my own little girl. "When are you due?"

"May twenty-eighth."

"A little spring bunny." I smiled, remembering the weight of Isabella in my arms, how perfect, how still. "You can have everything, Carrie. Everything."

She looked at me, puzzled.

"Dani, no..." Doc looked at me, understanding before she did and then her eyes widened.

"I want you to have it." I insisted, thinking of Isabella's crib, all her pink bedding and clothing and stuffed animals. "We'll paint your little girl's room pink and move all Isabella's things in here."

"Where will you stay?" Carrie asked.

"Until I leave for Italy..." I reached into my bra and pulled out my twenty-thousand dollar check. "I'll stay here in bed with you. Where else?"

Doc grinned. "I can live with that."

"What is this?" Carrie snatched the check and gaped at the amount.

"My divorce settlement." I tucked it back into my bra. "Mason was very generous."

"You're more generous." She tilted her face up and I kissed her softly. "Thank you."

"No." I nuzzled her throat and cuddled up with them both, my hand resting on her belly against Doc's. "Thank *you*. Both of you."

I had intended to give them a gift, the greatest gift I could imagine, but somehow, the Baumgartners had given me my life back, had actually brought me back to life. I closed my eyes and breathed in her scent, not quite recognizing the feeling that had overcome me. It seeped in slowly like honey around the edges of my consciousness, sticky and thick and sweet. It wasn't until I felt the tiniest little bump against my fingers, my eyes widening and my gaze meeting Doc's and then Carrie's in wonder, that I got it. The baby had kicked, letting us know she was alive and well, and that's when I understood what I was feeling.

I was happy.

GET FIVE FREE READS

Selena loves hearing from readers!
website: selenakitt.com
facebook: facebook.com/selenakittfanpage
twitter: twitter.com/selenakitt @selenakitt
blog: http://selenakitt.com/blog

Get ALL FIVE of Selena Kitt's FREE READS
by joining her mailing list!

MONTHLY contest winners!
BIG prizes awarded at the end of the year!

ABOUT SELENA KITT

Selena Kitt is a NEW YORK TIMES bestselling and award-winning author of erotica and erotic romance fiction. She is one of the highest selling erotic writers in the business with over a million books sold!

Her writing embodies everything from the spicy to the scandalous, but watch out-this kitty also has sharp claws and her stories often include intriguing edges and twists that take readers to new, thought-provoking depths.

When she's not pawing away at her keyboard, Selena runs an innovative publishing company (excessica.com) and book store (www.excitica.com).

Her books EcoErotica (2009), The Real Mother Goose (2010) and Heidi and the Kaiser (2011) were all Epic Award Finalists. Her only gay male romance, Second Chance, won the Epic Award in Erotica in 2011. Her story, Connections, was one of the runners-up for the 2006 Rauxa Prize, given annually to an erotic short story of "exceptional literary quality."

She can be reached on her website at
www.selenakitt.com

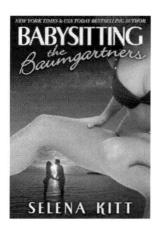

BABYSITTING THE BAUMGARTNERS
By Selena Kitt

Read the uber-hot, fun-in-the-sun, coming-of-age book that started it all!

Ronnie, now a college freshman, has been babysitting for the Baumgartners so long, she's practically a member of the family.

When Mrs. Baumgartner—who insists on calling her Veronica—invites Ronnie along on their yearly vacation, the nanny jumps at the chance.

There's no way she's going to turn down an opportunity to work on her tan in the Florida Keys with Doc and Mrs. B!

But Ronnie isn't the only one with ulterior motives.

The young co-ed discovers that the Baumgartners have wayward plans for their au pair that are going to lead places she could have only imagined.

Warning: This wicked hot sun and sand coming of age story will seduce you as quickly as the Baumgartners seduce innocent Ronnie and leave everyone yearning for more!

EXCERPT from
BABYSITTING THE BAUMGARTNERS:

When my legs felt steady enough to hold me, I got out of the shower and dried off, wrapping myself in one of the big white bath sheets. My room was across the hall from the bathroom, and the Baumgartner's was the next room over. The kids' rooms were at the other end of the hallway.

As I made my way across the hall, I heard Mrs. B's voice from behind their door. "You want that tight little nineteen-year-old pussy, Doc?"

I stopped, my heart leaping, my breath caught. *Oh my God.* Were they talking about me? He said something, but it was low, and I couldn't quite make it out. Then she said, "Just wait until I wax it for you. It'll be soft and smooth as a baby."

Shocked, I reached down between my legs, cupping my pussy as if to protect it, standing there transfixed, listening. I stepped closer to their door, seeing it wasn't completely closed, still trying to hear what they were saying. There wasn't any noise, now.

"Oh God!" I heard him groan. "Suck it harder."

My eyes wide, I felt the pulse returning between my thighs, a slow, steady heat. Was she sucking his cock? I remembered what it looked like in his hand—even from a distance, I could tell it was big—much bigger than any of the boys I'd ever been with.

"Ahhhh fuck, Carrie!" He moaned. I bit my lip, hearing Mrs. B's first name felt so wrong, somehow. "Take it all, baby!"

All?! My jaw dropped as I tried to imagine, pressing my hand over my throbbing mound. Mrs. B said something, but I couldn't hear it, and as I leaned toward the door, I bumped it with the towel wrapped around my hair. My hand went to my mouth and I took an involuntary step back as the door edged open just a crack. I turned to go to my room, but I knew that they would hear the sound of my door.

"You want to fuck me, baby?" she purred. "God, I'm so wet... did you see her sweet little tits?"

"Fuck, yeah," he murmured. "I wanted to come all over them."

Hearing his voice, I stepped back toward the door, peering through the crack. The bed was behind the door, at the opposite angle, but there was a large vanity table and mirror against the other wall, and I could see them reflected in it. Mrs. B was completely naked, kneeling over him. I saw her face, her breasts swinging as she took him into her mouth. His cock stood straight up in the air.

"She's got beautiful tits, doesn't she?" Mrs. B ran her tongue up and down the shaft.

"Yeah." His hand moved in her hair, pressing her down onto his cock. "I want to see her little pussy so bad. God, she's so beautiful."

"Do you want to see me eat it?" She moved up onto him, still stroking his cock. "Do you want to watch me lick that sweet, shaved cunt?"

I pressed a cool palm to my flushed cheek, but my other hand rubbed the towel between my legs as I watched. I'd never heard anyone say that word out loud and it both shocked and excited me.

"Oh God, yeah!" He grabbed her tits as they swayed over him. I saw her riding him, and knew he must be inside of her. "I want inside her tight little cunt."

I moved the towel aside and slipped my fingers between my lips.

He's talking about me!

The thought made my whole body tingle, and my pussy felt on fire. Already slick and wet from my orgasm in the shower, my fingers slid easily through my slit.

"I want to fuck her while she eats your pussy." He thrust up into her, his hands gripping her hips. Her breasts swayed as they rocked together. My eyes widened at the image he conjured, but Mrs. B moaned, moving faster on top of him.

"Yeah, baby!" She leaned over, her breasts dangling in his face. His hands went to them, his mouth sucking at her nipples, making her squeal and slam down against him even harder. "You want her on her hands and knees, her tight little ass in the air?"

He groaned, and I rubbed my clit even faster as he grabbed her and practically threw her off him onto the bed. She seemed to know what he wanted, because she got onto her hands and knees and he fucked her like that, from behind. The sound of them, flesh slapping against flesh, filled the room.

They were turned toward the mirror, but Mrs. B had her face buried in her arms, her ass lifted high in the air. Doc's eyes looked down between their legs, like he was watching himself slide in and out of her.

"Fuck!" Mrs. B's voice was muffled. "Oh fuck, Doc! Make me come!"

He grunted and drove into her harder. I watched her shudder and grab the covers in her fists. He didn't stop, though—his hands grabbed her hips and he worked himself into her over and over. I felt weak-kneed and full of heat, my fingers rubbing my aching clit in fast little circles. Mrs. B's orgasm had almost sent me right over the edge. I was very, very close.

"That tight nineteen-year-old cunt!" He shoved into her. "I want to taste her." He slammed into her again. "Fuck her." And again. "Make her come." And again. "Make her scream until she can't take anymore."

I leaned my forehead against the doorjamb for support, trying to control how fast my breath was coming, how fast my climax was coming, but I couldn't. I whimpered, watching him fuck her and knowing he was imagining me... *me!*

"Come here." He pulled out and Mrs. B turned around like she knew what he wanted. "Swallow it."

He knelt up on the bed as she pumped and sucked at his cock. I saw the first spurt land against her cheek, a thick white strand of cum, and then she covered the head with her mouth and swallowed, making soft mewing noises in her throat. I came then, too, shuddering and shivering against the doorframe, biting my lip to keep from crying out.

When I opened my eyes and came to my senses, Mrs. B was still on her hands and knees, focused between his legs—but Doc was looking right at me, his dark eyes on mine.

He saw me. For the second time today—he saw me.

My hand flew to my mouth and I stumbled back, fumbling for the doorknob behind me I knew was there. I finally found it, slipping into my room and shutting the door behind me. I leaned against it, my heart pounding, my pussy dripping, and wondered what I was going to do now.

YOU'VE REACHED

"THE END!"

Made in the USA
San Bernardino, CA
23 July 2019